"Luke O'Neil's stories are make me shout amen, call my mom Sometimes in the same sentence. Like nobody else working today, Luke articulates the agony of trying to live right now with a functioning heart, the anger of knowing right from wrong when one by one the people who taught you the difference turn out to have been joking. If you've been looking for the great art that bad times are supposed to bring about, look no further. Drywall is not that hard to patch."

—Dave Holmes, editor-at-large at Esquire

"Luke O'Neil has a degree in Massachusetts Studies and the human spirit. His stories imagine "a bill that will soon come due," in grief, in the wars we've waged on other countries and nature itself. His characters can't quit smoking or the hope that the bill might still be settled. O'Neil's stories will make you want to show emotion, even if your family didn't really do that shit."

—Daisy Alioto, co-founder, Dirt Media

"Luke O'Neil is the poet of our shared doom. It's good to know that at least we're all in this Hell World together."

—Maria Bustillos, Flaming Hydra

"What Luke O'Neil knows the answer to is a question both the straight world and the recovery community confronts every day—is anybody actually different from anybody else? And if so, what is addiction? The addict knows that being alive is the disease, a truth that science struggles to accept. *We Had It Coming* is not about suicide or addiction but the vivid, unmissable struggle of waking up, the only pain we are given, the first and last real gift. "

—Sasha Frere-Jones

"Luke O'Neil is one of the writers I admire the most—for the clarity with which he notices big things and small ones, for the righteousness and humor he brings to describing them, and for the stubborn humanity that runs through all of it."

—David Roth, editor and co-owner, Defector Media

"Like getting your ribs kicked in by a boot you can't help but notice is beautiful."

—Isaac Fitzgerald, *New York Times* bestselling author of *Dirtbag, Massachusetts*

"Reading these stories is like grabbing a beer with your friend who's smarter than you, and funnier than you, and knows way more than you do about how screwed up people are—and yet somehow, on the other side, he's made you feel better about the state of humanity, not worse."

—Rax King, author of the books *Tacky* and *Sloppy*

"Some writers describe, some convince, some guide. Luke just shows you what he saw, which is always somehow exactly right no matter how wrong it is and leaves you feeling as though you have just glimpsed something true. It is easy enough for a bad writer to use a thesaurus; it takes quite a good one to write whole symphonies in plain English. Luke is among the most talented writers around, if for no other reason that the man has a keener eye than he sometimes admits and he has a strong hatred of bullshit. No matter who you are as a reader, you'll find something you like in his writing."

—Linda Tirado, author of *Hand to Mouth: Living in Bootstrap America*

"Beautifully crafted collection of stories and essays that capture the times. Not without jolts of much-needed humor. Good stuff for bad times."

—Alex Winter

We Had It Coming

We Had It Coming
and other fictions

LUKE O'NEIL

OR Books
New York • London

© 2025 Luke O'Neil
Interior illustrations by Tyler Littwin. Cover-photo by Maryann O'Neil.

Published by OR Books, New York and London
Visit our website at www.orbooks.com

All rights information: rights@orbooks.com

All rights reserved. No part of this book may be reproduced or transmitted in any form or by any means, electronic or mechanical, including photocopy, recording, or any information storage retrieval system, without permission in writing from the publisher, except brief passages for review purposes.

First printing 2025

The manufacturer's authorised representative in the EU for product safety is Authorised Rep Compliance Ltd, 71 Lower Baggot Street, Dublin D02 P593 Ireland (www.arccompliance.com)

Typeset by Lapiz Digital. Printed by BookMobile, USA, and CPI, UK.

paperback ISBN 978-1-68219-669-4 • ebook ISBN 978-1-68219-670-0

I watched the sun rise
It was like a balloon
sent from Hell
straight to the moon
—Young Jesus, "Sunrise"

Why wouldn't I be trying to figure it out?
Everyone tells you that
Everyone tells you not to quit
I can't even see it to fight it
It looks like I'm not trying
I don't care what it looks like
—Songs:Ohia, "Ring the Bell"

The bad news is that it is real. The good news is that it is not eternal. Which is maybe just another cruel aspect of it.

No new word

There was a large bird perched atop the tallest tree in your neighborhood surveilling its domain and you two couldn't agree on whether or not it was a raptor of some kind or just a run of the mill crow. A flock of smaller birds nearby were agitated over its presence and yet they circled and circled closer to it caught in a whirlpool of their own panic. You worried for their safety. The big fella darted down so swiftly after one of them exploding into the thicket of a nearby bush and you said see I told you it's hunting something. It's going to get its ass. You picked up a rock and threw it into the leaves and scared them both off. A squirrel that had been minding its own business too. Why did you do that she said and you said you honestly did not know. You started to wonder if you had saved one bird's life or just starved another bigger bird. You thought maybe this is why God doesn't bother anymore.

Out of our misery

You saw a photo of panicked wild horses being chased by a helicopter. It loomed over them like a bird of prey in stark contrast against the backdrop of a scarlet setting sun.

The image crawled with you into bed and restless you fumbled for the plugged-in phone and poked around for more information and found an article that said that a dozen of the horses had died in the operation that day.

The rangers had been trying to round them up on federal land so they had made a break for it. One stallion fractured a leg and kept running on its other three for thirty six minutes it said which seemed so sad in its specificity.

No one wants the last few minutes of their life reported in the newspaper. Not even a horse.

Eventually they had to fly down closer to the ground when it had at long last collapsed and shoot it in the head. You presumed. It didn't say how they killed it. Probably like that.

Putting it out of its misery is what we call it when we kill an injured animal.

The story said some of the locals had named that particular horse Mr. Sunshine. It sounded made up but that's what the story said.

Four of the other horses ended up with broken necks. How does that even work? They must have been running so desperately to try to escape that their skeletons snapped under the weight of their stubborn wildness. A freedom we believed we had lent them. That wasn't ever ours to give.

Round Pond, Maine

The first thought is dad sprinting back and forth across 95 somewhere north of Boston. Like an old tabletop video game. Salvaging as many items of our wind-strewn clothing as he could. One of those tubes they make you stand in and the air blows the cash around. He must not have secured the suitcases well enough to the roof of the station wagon. Mitt Romney with a dog. Ours was safely inside though. An Irish setter named Arlo crouching in the backseat panting and staring dumbly at things he didn't understand and didn't need to anyway.

It doesn't seem worth it to me now. Risking all of that. But I've never had to pay to clothe children. Especially ones that aren't technically my own.

My mother's family had been coming summers to stay at a defunct cove-side motel in this no stoplight town since they were children. Then at a small house of their very own. Next door to one church and across the street from another. Imagine New England on a postcard. The one hundred year old general store. Lobster traps everywhere even on land. Fried clams and ice cream and cold sadness like the water a few inches beneath the parts the sun reaches.

Ok now imagine it all slightly poorer than what you were thinking. Just a town. A town in Maine. Sunburnt men in overalls who knew how to do things and then died early for having done them.

Over the years my grandmother took to decorating the house like a musty drawing room in a gothic romance. Velvet and lace and burgundy. A purposeful dimness to it. Miss Havisham's cake. A vampire with a rusted fishing boat he kept meaning to take out on an overcast day.

She'd go on to live out the rest of her days there mostly alone. Not the full rest of her days but the rest of them before the last of them. Cobwebs everywhere. A tiny bathroom my dad built under the stairs that he also built. No flushing allowed unless it was absolutely necessary. The thick beams of the roof jagged with nails older than all of us pushing outward at impossible angles like gnarled claws. I worried when I was young what would happen if everything tipped upside down.

Probably it was all beautiful once. Before I understood anything. Maybe I'm just remembering it in disrepair. The opposite of rose-colored glasses.

Nothing made my grandmother happier than any of us going to stay up there. Whether she was in residence or not.

You have to go up there.

My mother and my aunt still say that to me all the time.

You have to go up there.

Saying it how you think they are saying it. The accent.

My high school girlfriend and my college girlfriend and maybe my girlfriend after college I can't remember anymore and then the last girlfriend I will ever have fingers crossed. There's a picture of us sitting there on some early 2000s 4th of July. She's all of 22 years old perhaps. My grandmother and aunt had made us put on silly Uncle Sam hats and I pouted because I was the coolest young man alive. I was going to be The Strokes. But I did it nonetheless to please them and besides girls like it when you do things to please your grandmothers and aunts.

We were out on the porch overlooking the harbor a couple hundred yards away through a brush field that wanted scything and I wish I had now any idea what either of us were thinking then.

We have so much time left.

Something like that.

More likely not even being aware the meter was running. Joyriding in the taxi.

We watched The Sound of Music on VHS that night. I'm just thinking of that now as she walks in from work. What movie did we watch in Maine that one time I said and she said The Sound of Music without even thinking about it.

Another time we came up alone and I made her pad thai with tuna. Tuna from a can. She has never let me forget that and that is fine I have that one coming.

I'm fishing off the docks at the marina and failing at the fishing and watching some older boys catching and then torturing a fish and I never fished again after that.

Jabbing the hook around in its mouth mangling it. Laughing as if it were the funniest joke you'd ever heard. Going look at me I'm a fish in a sadistic ventriloquism. I wanted to jab their mouths and throw those kids into the water but I didn't do that because I was a chubby little baby.

Cousins and sisters and cousins jumping off an old mill pillar into a dark lagoon next to a once employed waterfall. Even the waterfalls out of work. Then drying off and lounging on its stones we imagined as a glamorous beach. An actual beach not very far off. Out by a sort of famous lighthouse one would drive along the curving coast to see if one were driving around here and looking for things to see. To kill time. To feel as if one were in Maine. Scare quotes Maine.

To kill a summer.

I climbed down once onto the sharp rocks by the lighthouse to breathe in the spray of the furious waves when my grandmother wasn't looking. Maybe because she told me so many times to never do it.

It doesn't seem worth it to me now. Risking all of that.

We're no longer children. Some of us have our own. Not me but some of us.

I couldn't handle that constant fear. That they could so easily be washed away any moment when you turned your back. Like I was asking for. I'm told there's a lot of joy in the endeavor of parenting but it cannot possibly compare to the agony of its ending.

There are big signs down by the water now warning people off. Some people's children aren't here anymore to read them.

I almost never climbed down onto any dangerous rocks ever again after one particular scare at the lighthouse until maybe twenty five years later. Ignoring a different sign this time by an entirely different ocean. A sudden tug and now being carried away I was reminded of the thrill seeking of youth but this time spoiled by an adult's awareness of the consequence. The one consequence that matters.

I wasn't actually thinking any of that at the time though that's a lie. I was thinking oh fuck oh God. Please no.

One single winter visit I can recall and never again after that. Having learned that lesson. So many different ways that water in one form or another wants to kill us. The snow isn't as bad now I'm told although that fact is bad in its own way.

A high school friends trip and walking down to the lobster shack swaggering like celebrities. In our stupid baseball caps. Girls. One of them was named Olive. I will never forget that for some reason. The stupid things that stick with us. She didn't want to kiss me and this was a revelation because almost everyone I had ever met in my life had wanted to kiss me.

A bachelor party with college buddies not long after graduation. Some of them jumped into the water off a bridge and had to claw their way up and out over the razor barnacled stones to get back to land. Their hands and feet red and raw. How that can be funny when you're a young man. The self-inflicted wounds that you still have the rest of your life to heal from. Guess I can't jack off for a while haha.

Like that.

A cousin's wedding at a dockside restaurant the next town over near the squat 17th century stone fort we used to run around inside of. Pretending to shoot the cannons at the French or the Natives or whoever it was they were shooting the cannons at back then. Something forced about this particular later in life trip though. Too old now to appreciate even the nostalgia which had been hammered and folded over and over so many years into a blunt flatness. Nostalgia for a prior nostalgia diminishing.

You have to go up there my mother said the other day and one thousand other days before that and I should but I'm not going to. It's too far away. Both meanings.

Another trip with my bandmates mid-twenties. Asking them not to bring drugs with us just for this one weekend. This is not a place where you do cocaine. I suppose a lot of people do heroin thereabouts now but less so then. One of them lied and said they scored on the way to fuck with me and I got so mad I pulled the car over and went and sat and watched a little league baseball game alone.

I knew things were heading in a bad direction with respect to all of that. Some people's children died but not me. Washed away.

We concocted a serial killer villain called the Bee Keeper that night after seeing a normal one (*or was he?*) on the main road into town and he haunted us that entire weekend even though we all knew that we were scaring ourselves. It didn't matter that the Bee Keeper wasn't real he became so when it got so dark the entire sky was stars and you could hear a twig snap. You could hear the silence of the two churches. What their emptiness implied.

The last time we were all there together my own family and the extended family we left my grandmother to float away into the water. It went smoothly. The spreading of her ashes. These sorts of things are more difficult than you think to get right.

Some of my nieces wrote letters to her in bottles and threw them out.

If I had written one I would have said I love you so much and I think about you almost every day but you fucked us all up so badly.

I swear to god she did but we love her all the same. Perhaps even more for it.

We are all so sick.

I don't know what else there was.

I wish now in this moment that I had held onto more of the memories. Had bundled them all close to my chest in the wind. But the highway is too broad and everything is moving with such speed.

How it is done

They told us that we were not killing him when it came time to turn off the machines but then what were we doing?

I do not know and I will never know and neither will you.

They said there was nothing left to be done anymore. All potential avenues had been explored. Somberly and politely and professionally they told us that. Touching our shoulders perhaps.

Shaking the doctor's hand like a salesman we were closing a deal with.

And this assemblage of children some of whom barely knew each other or barely even knew him were suddenly thrown together like a ragtag group in a heist movie except what we were stealing was a life.

Not really though they said.

They take you into some room they have around the corner from where whoever the person is is attached to the machine and they tell you what is happening and you're either the type to meticulously take notes to record what they're saying so you can try to logic your way out of the most unsolvable puzzle we have going or you're the kind that blacks out and everything they say dissipates into thin air.

There always has to be a captain in these scenarios. A reluctant captain. Alright. Alright. Duty is calling.

Probably that was me but I also remember thinking that this isn't even my ship. I don't know how to steer this thing.

I do not recommend the experience on the whole. Taking someone off of life support. I don't think I will ever get over it. Watching him die so slowly like that while still being very much alive in the counterbalance the entire time.

I'm very sorry if you understand this.

Wondering if he was conscious somewhere down in there screaming to be set free.

They told me that he was not. That he wasn't there anymore. Ok man then is he out back? Where the fuck did you put him? Who is that right there that I am looking at?

If I take you at your word that we are not killing him then what are we doing specifically?

A year later my estranged sister called on an anniversary we would now observe together forever.

Maybe we were siphoning out the suffering from his full tank and distributing it amongst ourselves she said. Each taking our fair share.

One of us greedier than the others and stashing a little extra for later.

I will swim to you

The five of us spread out a blanket on the grass and watched a band play Doobie Brothers covers in a park by the shore. Later I had my first swim in the ocean of the season. I tip-toed into the water with our friend's daughter who is maybe six. I don't know how to tell how old kids around that age are. She reached out gently for my hand and I took it gently in turn and it broke my heart gently. I didn't even know we were close like that. I kept looking back to land like is this ok? Am I doing this correctly? Worrying that a rogue wave from the movie they filmed near here would swell out of nowhere and suck her out into the depths and pull me into a different kind of drowning. I gambled anyway because she seemed fearless and we waded on acting silly about how cold it was but determined to keep going. To have gotten it done. I thought of a picture I had seen earlier of a child's ruined body in a shape I had never seen a human body in before. Not even in a movie. I don't know how old she was either. Maybe six. A family of ducks were swimming a little further out and my brave friend said we should go out to the duckies and try to save them because there might be sharks but I told her that they were too far away for us to be able to help. We couldn't swim fast enough to catch up to them I said and I knew she didn't believe me.

They can fly away if they want to I told her. Saying something true but lying. I looked back to the shore one more time and saw her father waving to us and we stood there shivering in the absence of current under a completely silent and empty sky.

The vacuum

I sat out in one of the heavy beach-blue beach chairs it took us forever to assemble that one frustrating day when we loved each other and watched the trees not move at all. Like the TV screen of late when it freezes for hours. I wanted for their summer browning and deathly still leaves to waver an inch. At least some sign of movement.

Place your ear to an injured person's chest.

No idea in this case how to perform CPR on trees and all of everything.

Sitting in this very spot this very rough hour two rough summers ago so many different types of insects would have been crawling over and onto and into me that I could have convinced myself I was lost in a bad trip. But then just like that I would have snapped to and remembered what the outside is. Or used to be.

It had been sort of a last call deal for them it turned out. The bugs. Today my ankles and forearms unbitten. My God you can miss anything when it's gone. Any fucking thing.

Do you remember this? Beach-burned and heat-drowsy scraping the unclipped talons of one foot against the red welts on the back of the other in a sweating bed.

You were inside cooking sausages and onions I couldn't smell even with the windows open. Not real sausages. Not real onions. For our health you lied to me. For morale. With nothing to possibly gain from the effort besides more of us and more of this.

Yesterday you disassembled our ancient vacuum. Piece by piece. To figure out if it was worth saving. Cleaned every purple plastic part of it. I thought of a sniper breaking down his rifle.

There must be dust in here from five apartments ago you said.

You had never cleaned it this thoroughly before you said.

Inside of its barrel organs was so much shedded tangled hair that had fallen off of us and the last of the dogs that we had once named. That had been bred for us to die. Curled and compacted into solid hardened knots like a cancer. We carried all of it from home to home without even knowing it. Everywhere we had to move away from. Smuggled in our baggage like a stowaway.

I thought for the first time in years of all of the abandoned boxes of my old books in a basement somewhere else someone else has to worry about now. Some other guy. Watching a tree that was his new problem in a spot where I would have been sitting.

I'd have written this all better if I still had those books to thumb through for inspiration. Years ago out in some healthier greener yard. The bugs would be eating me alive out there. I'd want them all fucking dead.

How good we had it

Planes were falling from the sky and the sky itself was falling but didn't the driveway still need shoveling? Salt for the icy steps. The kitchen sink full again too. And every day a new reminder that crying can get you anything you want in the world if it's the right kind of crying. Tears of men weak enough to do grievous harm. I'm told that we can't post our way out of fascism but they quite literally posted us right into it. Just another one of the many unfair things about posting and fascism. I watched a Family Feud the other night where Steve told one of the teams that they didn't give him the answers on his card beforehand but he damn well knew what the answers were not. One of two scenarios have presented themselves which is that everything gets so bad so quickly that a sufficient response becomes inevitable or else they only get just so bad overtime that we can keep putting our duty off until it is no longer ours. I pick up my phone every five minutes expecting it to tell me something good about the world and I thought of a night some friends and I crawled around on all fours looking for crumbs of cocaine that had been accidentally blown off the table into the carpet. I've been asking myself just how it is that a person can go about their day to day life at a time like this and I keep coming back to another question which is how did we ever convince ourselves we had the right to do so before?

The known world

Overnight her car's spider had erected yet another elaborate web on the side view mirror. Must have spent hours on the thing it looked like. She thought of brushing the entire mess off once again with the ice scraper from the back seat but then felt a pang of conscience. It couldn't have been eating well lately what with her wiping its labors to hell every day. Going around cutting the lines of a village's lobster traps. She turned the engine over and glanced at it perched there motionless and tense. Two spiders accounting for the reflection actually. Waiting in their own ornate webs in reverse. Famished in a trap they had both set for themselves.

How to write

So much of our great art is born of youthful heartbreak which is unfair because it puts you at a disadvantage creatively not to mention marketing-wise if you're aging in a happy marriage. One of the main things we're supposed to want.

Eventually the last and ultimate heartbreak starts to crest on the horizon though and the creative impulse is refreshed.

Time to be taught and to try to teach the only lesson there is to people too young to believe it.

The rules

I was fighting fascism with the power of love and kindness and just really getting my ass handed to me. A total bloodbath. The referee would have stepped in by now but they had knocked him out with a steel chair. The only others watching were either fascists themselves or the people trying to fight fascism with the power of love and kindness and they weren't having a great go of it either. I kept trying to explain in between haymakers that we were better than this and on top of that it wasn't likely to be ruled on favorably as far as the courts. None of it helped. I was on my knees now bleeding profusely from the mouth and nose. It spilled out of me onto the snow in a pattern that if you sort of squinted at it from the right vantage looked like a cartoon heart. See that I pointed. Look how beautiful the world can be I tried to say through my broken teeth. Alright well now he was pulling out a gun. I didn't think we were allowed do that.

The fullest extent of the law

The morning after the wildfires had spread widely enough that they begged addressing the mayor stood up outside of the charred strip mall where we used to get takeout Korean and assured the public that any looters would be dealt with in the harshest possible fashion. Much like she had said before with respect to the floods.

The tableau was almost beautiful. Ash falling like snowflakes and the heat of the flames over the hill glowing like Christmas. Someone must have set that up.

Five of them had been arrested already she said this time and the last time and the next. Criminals who had come from outside of the city she said. The councilors joined along in chorus after her in their own respective speeches. Both ally and enemy alike. A switch having flipped in all of their brains when they realized that they could not shoot and could not arrest fire or water or wind. After that they were out of ideas. Punishment being the only tool they had ever wielded.

I was sitting on the foot edge of a bad bed in a motel seventy five miles south while the kids were outside bothering the buttons of an emptied out soda machine. Each of us wishing for a different kind of miracle.

I checked out of habit to see if they had a Bible in the drawer.

This is not who we are she said.

What was it exactly that they were supposed to be looting here? Were they stuffing their pockets with fistfuls of ash?

There was nothing that we had left behind that anyone could take from us in any way that mattered anymore. It all belonged to the fire now. Probably always did.

Believing you will receive

I was out on the porch in the dark with a friend who had stopped by to tell me he was getting a divorce. No no no he didn't want to come inside and disturb the kids he said. Out here is fine he said. I brought out a couple of ice cold cold ones and listened to a story about the collapse of an entire world. I confess I teared up more than he did.

Then again it was sudden news to me. You would figure it had settled in for him by now. Hopefully being one of the first people to know about the slow dissolution of his own marriage.

A person can become accustomed to almost any kind of pain. Novelty is pain's cruelest device.

We hugged differently than we had ever hugged.

A decent enough man will hug his friends routinely albeit quickly and percussively but there is still a kind of hug we keep in reserve for when it is called for.

A special occasion when the rare bottle is brought up from the cellar and decanted.

We bullshitted for a while as the night bugs screamed in car alarm. Like someone was breaking into every tree and bush and nest on the block one by one. How panic is infectious like that. How it pollutes. How animals flee. Birds explode into the sky in unison at a rifle's crack.

No there was nothing to be done about it he said after some interviewing. Wasn't sure if he wanted there to be anymore.

I was trying to solve it for him like a 1,000 piece puzzle I wasn't even at the table doing. Shouting out instructions blindly from the other room.

Everything was going to be alright he said.

Trying to reassure me more than himself it seemed like.

He was walking around downtown earlier trying to clear his head and he saw the funniest thing he said. He passed by a wedding in the park where the groom was reciting the lyrics to Nothing Else Matters as part of his vows. But doing it in the thickest Massachusetts accent he'd ever heard.

That's honestly so beautiful to me I said.

I didn't know whether to cry or laugh he said.

He sounded like you he said.

No matter how far I sang and we each laughed a half of a laugh.

Love is the only thing that is real he said in a suddenly different voice and I wasn't sure how to respond to that.

I said damn right.

A subdued damn right. A mournful damn right.

Looks like the pope is about to die he said and I said that I had heard that.

They put out a statement asking for everyone's prayers he said. But if he can't even get his calls picked up then what were any of us supposed to do about it?

Then we talked about how much the Red Sox fucking sucked for a while.

After he had retreated to his suddenly unfamiliar home I went back into my too familiar home and debriefed my wife and told her I was gonna go back and sit out on the porch for a while to decompress. I got myself another can and turned my playlist on shuffle.

It don't make you do a thing it just lets you.

The next morning my doctor's office emailed to remind me that my upcoming free annual preventative health exam may not technically be free as per recent federal guidelines. The appointment is this week and I'm worried she's going to tell me all my numbers look fine. That there is nothing wrong with me that I have the power to fix.

Just over the hill deer were busy shedding their velvet. Agitating their antlers against the bark and brush and stripping off the protective layer messily and bloodily.

Have you seen this? The draped flesh hanging like red rags off of their sharpened points. Doing it over and over again every year.

Had he not already existed you would have had to invent the Devil Himself if you ever came across such a sight in the woods.

Maybe that's where they originally got the idea I don't know.

Sometimes they eat it too. So that nothing is wasted. And later in the year when the antlers fall off completely other smaller animals congregate and each in turn eat of them for their calcium and protein and to shave down their own constantly growing teeth.

And it's a chilly dry morning at the end of the mildest summer I can remember and I can't fully appreciate its comfort because it all feels like a bill that will soon come due.

I'm not saying you shouldn't try to help

I was looking at my phone on the couch when D___ looked up from her phone on the couch and she goes please don't ever open the door for a strange woman if she arrives asking for help. This was the second time she had asked this favor of me in the span of a few weeks and so I figured it must be something going around on her version of the phone that I wasn't privy to on my version of the phone. The way her world is infinitesimally different from mine and yours is from hers and so on and so on. Next thing one of us is trying to convince the other that *they* are lying to *us* about the war.

Not just disputing facts and motivations and conspiracies I mean but suggesting that it isn't even happening at all.

Even if it's a woman who seems like she's in distress she said and I said I don't know if I can agree to these terms on a blanket policy level. I think it's going to have to be on a case by case basis I said. I'll kind of be freelancing on the matter I said and she said you can say you'll call someone for help obviously just don't invite them inside.

I think that's the rule for vampires not ladies I said and she said vampires aren't real but this is.

Our niece had slept over a few nights before and she's at that age where she's starting to watch horror movies and loves to talk about them almost to scare herself on purpose in the daylight when it's safer. To poke her feelers out into what the frightening world can sometimes be in the way that kids do. She asked me what my favorite horror movie ever was and I thought about it for a minute or two and couldn't decide on just one like I was worried about insufficiently impressing this child with my refined taste and I said well I will tell you one horror movie that has stuck with me because of how abject and mean it was and that is House of 1000 Corpses. It was made by Haverhill Massachusetts' own Robert Bartleh Cummings I said and she said she hadn't heard of it. I thought about pulling up More Human Than Human for her on YouTube to illustrate what the nineties were like for me and her parents more than anything but instead I said have you ever heard of the band Wet Leg and she said what and I said have you ever heard of the band Wet Leg and she said yeah. She said that she had heard of them. D___ said what band are you talking about and I sang a little of Chaise Longue with the cute accent and everything and she said oh right.

I don't think I've ever spent any real time in Haverhill despite having a degree in Massachusetts Studies (unaccredited) although I know it's a decently large river milltown that has probably seen better days even though it was founded something like four hundred years ago. To be frank I imagine the days were worse then no matter what it's like there now.

No one ever says a town has seen worse days it's always the other way around.

I have been to or at least driven through Lawrence and North Andover and Methuen and Salisbury and Amesbury and definitely Newburyport all of which are basically on the Merrimack River which dumps out into the Atlantic where they would have been shipping the lumber and whatever else it was they processed in Haverhill for all those years. I wonder how much it would fuck up the course of human history if I travelled back in time and played the good people of colonial Haverhill a few cuts off of White Zombie's Astro Creep: 2000. Maybe instead of gratitude for introducing them to the concept of riffs they would just kill me instantly with an ax and I'd be there bleeding into the soil I was meant to bleed into much later on going the gag wasn't worth it. I've made a mistake here.

Why was the movie scary my niece asked and I said it wasn't so much that it was scary like you're thinking but more that it was a cruel movie that reveled in its stylized torture which I'd rather not have to watch happening if I had my way. In real life or in fiction.

Then I remembered the plot of the film is set into motion by a woman in supposed distress flagging down a car on a desolate road and asking for help from Dwight Schrute and all them. The actual Dwight Schrute would've been fucked in that scenario too although he would've known his way around a rural farm a little better than those guys in the movie you would think.

She asked if we could watch Human Centipede later because her dad would never let her and I said no but just as much for me as for her.

It's not that her dad wouldn't let her she said but that he didn't want to watch it with her either and she was too scared to watch it alone.

Poltergeist I thought later. It's Poltergeist.

I was younger than her when I saw it for the first time so maybe it doesn't hold up anymore. The doll and the TV and all of that. I'd kick that stupid fucking doll 50 yards through the uprights today.

I'm not entirely sure if we're meant to be judging horror movies on their technical prowess as films in terms of acting and story and direction and lighting and costuming and setting or instead just how embedded they get inside of us for the rest of our lives which seems like a stronger metric in my estimation.

Haunted house films have been scary forever for obvious reasons but I don't think I appreciated until recently how much worse it would be if it were the haunted home you had a haunted thirty year lease out on as opposed to some other random fucked up ghost house that wasn't your problem otherwise. The eccentric guy trapping you there or daring you to stay overnight. Aside from the ghouls there is the matter of the bank to contend with. I can't even get my bank to stop charging me three bucks every time I need to take out a twenty at the 7-Eleven for scratchies.

What are you looking at D___ asked me a couple days later and I swiped away from a picture of Pete Buttigieg eating a shredded up Cinnabon like a buffalo wing and lowered my phone and said nothing and she didn't say anything to follow up so I picked my phone back up and pulled up the picture of Pete Buttigieg eating a shredded up Cinnabon like a buffalo wing again.

Why did you tell me not to let a woman into the house I asked her.

I didn't say don't let a woman into the house.

What did you say?

I said that just so you know if a woman ever runs up frantically to the door and is knocking on the door saying she's in danger and she needs to come in call the police immediately and then tell her that you called the police and they'll be there in a minute and don't let her into the house. I think that it could be a scam and you could be putting yourself into danger.

What is the scam though?

Well you let her in and she's like armed and then there's like a guy or two outside and she like you know she's like gonna let them in and then who knows what they wanna do with you. Kidnap you. Murder you. Tie you up.

Haha.

Haha.

Why is it funny I said.

I don't know. It's not really she said. I just laughed because you did. It made me nervous.

But where did you see all of this?

I've heard a few different stories. Probably mostly on TikTok. True crime sort of stories like now let's learn about the horrible fate of so and so. There are true things that happen. It can also happen when you're in your car. Like you can be driving along in a desolate area and you see a woman in the street and she's like waving you down like please help.

Like in a movie.

No like in real life.

Do you think people are gassing themselves up a little bit too much with this shit? People on TikTok who have seen too many documentaries.

Personally I've never done any research but I think you could look into it and find out that this has actually happened to people.

I'm sure that it has happened but… It's also possible that someone might hit a golf ball at the course we go walking by and it shoots off in a weird direction and hits me in the head and my pants fall down and everyone sees my little flapping penis spinning around like a pinwheel. Do you ever worry about that?

There's really not much you can do to prevent that! The thing I'm talking about all you would have to do is go I'm very sorry but I can't help you because I could potentially be putting myself into danger. I don't know you. I don't trust you.

I guess it has something to do with me being a man and you being a woman right?

Absolutely. 100%. There is that. You know as a woman I have a lot more fears about my bodily autonomy and my safety and you know... Although that woman and her accomplices? It doesn't matter. They could still hurt you if this were to happen to you.

Well obviously I could be overpowered.

The reason I tell this to you specifically is that you always want to help people and I just want you to know that it's good and kind of you to want to help people but you also should make sure you are protecting yourself. And me.

Yeah that's fine.

I'm not saying you shouldn't try to help. But I would not open the door to a stranger that was knocking in the middle of the night.

I didn't know this was all happening in the middle of the night.

Obviously.

What's the scariest horror movie you've ever seen?

Oh um for some reason I want to say The Babadook. That one scared me a lot. I don't know why. I think it was the specific night we watched it. It was a scary night. For us. And you fell asleep instantly.

It's *about grief* I said.

Yes I know that. I couldn't sleep and there was a creature in our room when I tried to sleep. Waiting there. Midsommar too. The end of it.

That was really creepy. Look at these bombed out buildings I said gesturing toward the muted TV.

That's awful. A year it's been.

A year.

These poor people.

There were some guys on my phone today trying to convince each other that none of it was happening.

What? Why?

I don't know. To feel something. To feel different. Listen to me though I said. I think I'm gonna do it. Let the lady in.

Then you're putting me in danger because you want to try to be the savior for someone! You know bad things happen to people that are trying to be kind all the time.

Is she hot?

Who?

The girl at the door.

I don't know if she's hot.

What if she's very old? That could also be a motivating factor.

You just can't let anybody into the house.

What about a repairman?

If you called them that's fine!

What about... *The Hangman*?

No don't start that again.

What if it's ol' Jack The Smiling Hangman himself coming round rattling his bag of teeth?

No. That's a no brainer. That's a closed door scenario.

What if he's very charming and he just wants to show me I don't know...

That's how they get you!

...his set of steak knives.

No! I don't even open the door for anyone. This summer someone came and knocked on the door and they wanted to talk to me about electricity or something and I said no thank you. I was mad. It was a guy. Men should realize we're not comfortable opening our doors to you. But also don't do it for a woman either.

What if she has really big tits?

No! That's even worse. But you know what someday I could be in really big trouble and I might have to go run down the street and knock on a door.

And they won't let you in. How do you like that?

I don't. I'll think about this conversation and then I'll be dead. The zombies got me because they wouldn't open the door because that person's wife told them don't ever open the door. So you're damned if you do and damned if you don't I guess.

I feel like I'm pretty street smart I said. You don't have to... Why are you laughing?

Haha.

Haha.

I think you're street smart too. I just thought this was one thing you might not know about.

What?

This scam.

Why are you laughing?

I don't know why! I just thought you might not know this is a thing that uh… bad players do.

What was that home invasion movie? Funny Games? Where they tie the family up and torture them? Did you watch that?

No that would be terrifying to me because I have a huge fear of… Everyone in my family … my kinfolk all have a fear of …

For some reason it sounds racist when you say kinfolk.

Sorry. Well my family growing up all had a fear of home invasion.

But nothing ever happened?

Well nothing yet. Not until you came onto the scene!

I'm opening the door to every wastrel who comes along. Motel 6 ass.

Haha that's right.

Like in that show we've been watching. The monsters pretend to be somebody you know

That's exactly what I mean.

Let us in dear. I'm your old granny. Or the one where she's like I just want to kiss you to the guy and he gets horny and lets her in and she kisses him for a minute then bites his face off.

That's right. That's why you never get horny. Not once.

Well that's why I was asking about the situation with her tits. I don't think that's going to happen in this town by the way.

You don't think anyone in this town has big tits?

No I meant the uh...

Something bad could happen anywhere. Look at where I grew up. The past two months two horrible unthinkable crazy violent tragedies have happened. The lady with her kids. We never would've thought that was going to happen. But the truth is bad things can happen anywhere. And just think about the other day when I was walking home from the car shop... whatever it's called.

Garage.

The garage. It was in broad daylight and a man was harassing me from his car following me. I never thought anything like that would happen.

That was fucked up. I gotta find that guy.

The other day I thought I was going to see him somewhere. At the gym.

I'm gonna invite myself into his house.

Don't! It works both ways. You don't let people in and you don't go in.

I'll put a wig on. Like Bugs Bunny. Alright what was your horror movie besides Babadook?

Well I don't watch a lot because they scare me and I can't go to sleep at night then you always fall asleep before me. Which actually would be a good thing if someone came knocking on the door because then I could handle it!

I would know. I would sense it. Hey come on in everyone!

I know you would! This is why I tell you because this is how it plays out in my mind. I am in my slumber and you wake up to the knocking and you go down and you of course let the person in and they've got a gun on you and they tie you up and let in the other people then I wake up like didn't we talk about this? This is the one thing I told you not to do!

Ok fine I won't do it I said but I was sort of lying and the matter being settled for now we got quiet and I looked out the window and there was a young girl walking down the street that looked like my niece and I thought she was coming up to the front door but she wasn't she was just walking with her family down the road. All of them bundled up for the cold. Going to wherever it is people end up when you can't see them anymore.

Wait. It was Fire in the Sky I said. I just remembered. Nothing was ever scarier to me than that. Did you see that one I said and she said she hadn't.

I picked up my phone and there was the picture of Pete Buttigieg eating a shredded up Cinnabon like a buffalo wing and I felt uneasy about it like it was following me around. There should be a way to mute a photo I thought.

I looked out the window again and no one was there.

After that I saw a picture with the caption "Boy cleaning slaughterhouse in Nebraska. Photo provided by Department of Labor investigators. He was employed by a cleaning company owned by Blackstone private equity firm" and they have his face blurred out in the post because it's considered bad form to share pictures of children online. You wouldn't want them to be exposed to harm like that. There was another boy in the story who was thirteen years old and it said he worked twelve hours a day six days a week on an egg farm in Michigan.

"I'd like to go to school, but then how would I pay rent?" the boy told the newspaper.

It didn't say if either of the boys had a favorite horror movie.

Next thing I saw a tweet from some random guy that had posted a picture of tents on the sidewalk in San Francisco and he wrote "We live down the street from this encampment. They are still there and have shown no signs of leaving. Meanwhile, people pay $30k for their kids to go to school with these people looking on…" and I thought one of these things is more profane than the other one man.

Sometimes I feel like I was born with all of the regret I was meant to have gradually accumulated over the course of my entire life already fully loaded into my software from day one. A WeTransfer file someone dropped into my crib when my mother wasn't looking and my fat little baby finger downloaded it.

I don't know how to do computer metaphors but you understand me right?

Maybe it's getting the bill before you've even eaten the meal. And with that the knowledge that I could perhaps prevent some of the regret by altering my behavior but with a stone unwillingness to do so. Like the chef comes out and tells you the entree you're about to order will be raw and undercooked and will likely sicken you but you don't believe them and are hungrier than ever for the worm meat now.

You take a little picture of the worm meat on your phone and the lighting is off so you try one more time.

D___ was over there on the couch looking at her phone and laughing. No one was outside. No one was knocking at the door. No one was killing anyone.

What's funny now I said and she goes it's nothing really. Just a funny picture. Here she said as she was texting me the link. I already knew what it was going to be.

It was incredibly lucky that I was here

I'm looking at a video of ___ on stage right now. He sounds like he sounds. Like how you remember him sounding from one day ago when he was still alive. The casually delivered growl of a man who has lived and also very much always almost not lived throughout most of that living.

I must have seen this at the time. I was still very young at this point even as old as I am now but this show was a big deal for the people like me watching and an even bigger deal for the bands playing although probably not for ___ who didn't seem to be impressed by much of anything.

Sorry I'm making a singer's life about me but that is the deal. They sing about their life and I take it to be about my life and then I write about it and the people reading that take it to be about theirs.

People love to deify a person on the day they die but then it diminishes incrementally over time. Unless they were a very big deal. Our man here seems like the type of guy whose stature will grow posthumously I'd imagine. People who sing about death and pain a lot become more important when they're gone because now it seems like they've completed the final course prerequisite.

That's a dangerous pattern for a certain type of person to notice.

Hold on let me look up how old he was at the time of that performance.

He was twenty eight. Old enough to not be too overwhelmed by it all but still.

God his voice sounds so good. Jagged but strong.

Let's make a conservative estimate and say at a clip of around 20 smokes a day times almost 11,000 days since then that his voice was about 220,000 cigarettes younger than the day he died.

He's got a black eye and he looks like the type of guy who would have a black eye as a matter of principle.

Everyone loves this song. Everyone loves it and it's still underrated.

The day before the band had been in a bar brawl and their drummer fucked up his shoulder which accounts for why there's some other guy sitting in. ___ is wearing a very nice black leather jacket and his hair looks clean and I'm wondering if he washed it because he was going to be on TV and if so that breaks my heart a little bit. If he had at one point wanted to look his best for when people remembered him later on in these kinds of videos. The place he still exists.

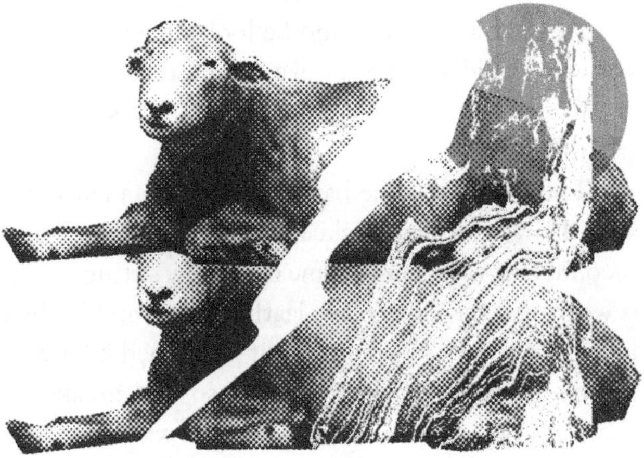

One more time around

I was so sick. Absolutely fucked. No two ways around the thing. Believe me I puked and cried over it and consulted every hack I could find on the computer and then after all of that there was nothing to be done. My close personal friends the doctors had become more aloof to me every passing month. Distancing themselves from my stench. Like I had done something wrong to them. Which I had. I had failed them in fact in my unhealing.

A coach doesn't exactly blame you per se for missing the final shot but they do remember how hard you had or had not practiced all season. Whether or not you had listened. Paid attention to fundamentals.

So I had had my exit all planned out. They were supposed to put my good headphones on me and then stick me with it. The nurses would never promise no matter how many times I double checked that it would all happen precisely as choreographed but if all went well it was meant to catch final purchase right around when Chris Cornell comes back in after the solo on Slaves & Bulldozers and then I was supposed to have been well on my way to well on my way home.

Counting all the hands I shook on the way out the door.

My dear poor aunt.

My bunny.

Instead I woke up. I don't know how much longer after.

Maybe one hundred years.

That's stupid. There was no shot of space ships out the window when I came to. No robots lumbering around. Just boiling old Boston out there.

I was probably a day at most in my halfness.

I don't blame them too much. These nurses are very overworked. What with the heat on top of everything else.

I asked the first nurse who curtained in what day it was and then how hot it was and neither of her answers made sense.

She lied to me and said it was only 90 degrees.

I remember when my own father died after trying so many times to get it right or at least to get the damned hateful business over with that the nurses had told me what a charmer he had been. Right up until it happened. How he was such a big flirt. But I didn't want that on my record on the way out the door. I was still together enough to know they didn't want any of that from me either. And besides what good was it going to do me if they had?

To see a pretty lady smile though. Now that's something to live for. One more time.

Perhaps I should have flirted more. With my shit tube sticking out of me.

In terms of what it felt like? Well I had this shivering vision of someone attempting a push-up.

A ten year old boy trying to impress his father and failing at it.

Alright well you'll get better at it boy you just have to keep trying.

Now go again.

Right now.

But think of that entire operation flipped upside down in the situation at hand regarding me. My ghost strained for planking vertical lift-off up and out of my meat and then fell back almost instantly toward gravity in its exhaustion.

I had been kind of hoping that God or One of All of Them would have been there for a pep talk. Maybe one of his Lesser Guys I assume that they have. Handing out cups of water along the final marathon route. The least senior one would have been fine with me. I didn't need anything special or fancy. But no there was none of that. Could just be I didn't get that far into the process.

I'm embarrassed to say I did kind of believe just a little bit that He was going to greet me immediately though. Our Father yes but also my specific father too.

Now try again.

Right now.

One or both of them there to kick me in the ass then usher me up and into wherever they make you wait for processing. To make sure you have your papers in order.

The secretary lady going do you need anything? Water?

It could be a secretary guy you know what I mean.

Instead I was still down here and it was just this unfamiliar nurse hovering over me with a paper cup.

I don't suppose that we will need to need water there. Although why did they make it so we need to need water here? That didn't have to be a requirement. That was decided.

I drank from her water.

What had I done that was all that bad in the scheme of it all? In the balance of every single thing that had ever been done? I had worked as long as I could. My kids were good kids. No kids of their own yet but that was fine. That didn't knife me in my heart. That didn't cut into my bowels.

Their mother didn't despise me. Hadn't come to see me off as far as I could tell but.

So it was like.

You know how they sometimes are set to launch a shuttle into space but the weather is coming from the wrong direction and everyone agrees to try again tomorrow?

At the end of it all it was my spirit misfiring. On top of everything else to do with my body.

A lighter you left out in the rain overnight.

***

If they are blessed a person gets to lay there waiting for it to come for a good long while. Not too long mind you. Not that. Nobody wishes for that.

Whoever is left to give a shit or feel as if they have to present as giving a shit stops by and most often doesn't know how to act no matter how many times they've gone through it and no matter how many times we all have gone through it. Catholics I mean. Other kinds of people too I'm sure. Although a lot of them seem less afraid of it than we do.

The one single thing that definitely happens.

Bringing gifts instead of overt love because they only know how to socialize with the living. People with a future. The past is something you contend with alone.

Flowers too. Thank you very much to all or some of you for letting me watch this series of bouquets die. I did not need the additional metaphor to get the gist of things.

Nobody ever talks about how bad flowers inevitably come to smell. It's always the other end of the operation. The start of something beautiful.

***

But let us say this time in this one instance someone caresses your cheek with the back of their hand. Holds your hand. For a good long while. A real handhold.

When was the last time you tenderly held hands with your parents or grandparents without feeling self conscious about it?

Did I ever tenderly hold the hand of my sisters or brothers?

Surely I must have for some number of years and then never did so again. Maybe when our own father died. A parent's death infantilizes you to the point that it's all instinctual again briefly. All of it. The entire history of everything. You are a one-celled organism and then you are a majestic blue whale and then you are nothing.

For the duration of his passing we were mostly once again children. An unspoken agreement. We had signed some papers in the hospital and maybe that was part of it. No one knew what we were signing exactly. We didn't read the fine print.

I'm not going to be on the hook for paying for this I remember my brother saying. It was hot that day too but not like it is now. A previous heat that you could make jokes about.

A motherly passing is an entirely different thing. No one can take that. The symmetry of her life beginning and ending in a hospital bed.

Your life I mean. She had an entire short life before you existed.

Pretend it's not real.

It wasn't real.

I need to pretend harder.

You can touch a dying loved one in such a way that you never once touched them before in your entire life. Especially a father. You can kiss them on the forehead and there they still are after having been kissed by their son. Or whoever you are. Unmoved and unmoving. Swaddled like a newborn. Not going to fuss with something in the other room. Not going to take the dog for a walk. Not going out to the garage to fuck around with this or that. Probably unaware the kiss had even happened but you never know and I guess that's the only part that matters. That's why you do it. You do not and we do not ever know. Maybe the kisses are like cheers from the crowd to an athlete. All of what they need to ascend. To prove they earned it.

Then they get to drink the water.

***

Later or maybe before and I'm blinking my eyes wet and there was the local news on the TV in the corner of the room blurry and they were interviewing kids about the heat and how their school didn't have air conditioning and then a mother came on saying they were handing out popsicles to them at recess and then another mother came on and was pissed off about the free popsicles.

I glanced out the window and still no spaceships. A little deflated. One would have wanted to at least have lived to have seen that.

Wait where were my damned kids?

The boy was supposed to have been here to hold my hand throughout the procedure and perhaps steal a kiss on my forehead and the girl was going to contend with the money end of it but ok fine hold on now here he came shouldering back into the room like a sitcom neighbor with a look like uh oh and he said he had gone out for a drink and I could tell he felt bad about it so I let it slide for now for as long as I had forever. I would want a drink were it my own father I had to watch fail to leave properly. If the shoe were on the other foot. Which it had been. I remember doing that now. At a bar outside of MGH. Pretending none of it was real. The one single thing that definitely happens. Not even that hot out that late August. It was going to be the fall before we knew it.

Our time is up

She had therapy in a couple hours so she was running lines in the car trying to come up with some fresh bits or epiphanies. So that they would have something novel to talk about this week. To avoid belaboring the singular thing she was so sickened of confessing to. To not have to admit out loud that actually nothing had changed despite prior promises to the contrary. Not so much because the therapist would have to hear it all again but that she would have to hear herself saying it.

Still the same fuck up from last time.

It felt so embarrassing to have to do that. Like showing up to a friend's house with a vase of housewarming flowers every week then taking it home and coming back again. Wilting a little more with each iteration until they're foul.

A house cat dropping the same decomposing mouse at your feet over and over forever.

Look what I've done.

Worse than either of those things though because she was paying a lot of money for the privilege.

Thinking over and over:
I suffer no injury that I have not done to myself.
Like a mantra.
I suffer no injury that I have not done to myself.
Maybe that was a step forward?
Realizing how lucky she was that that was true.
Mostly true.

Currently true.

A sort of gratitude that no one was conspiring to harm her.

Mostly no one.

Currently no one.

Self-annihilation being a luxurious problem to have compared to how so many others suffer.

Are made to suffer.

Although when it's someone else coming after you at least you have the option of running.

Nothing was funny anymore

It was my turn to finally bump into one of these shitty robots out in the wild. Staggering down the sidewalk like a drunk. The robot not me.

Ok also me.

My buddies and I had been betting on who could go the longest without spotting one for months now. I guess the whole operation had finally made it to my town as these things happen. I texted the group chat to let them know I was tapping out and they roasted me and then it settled down after nothing was funny anymore. One of them asked what I thought of it on account of all the build up on the news and I said you guys were right all along. It looks like a piece of shit. Like vermin.

Doesn't look like vermin per se but looks the way vermin makes you feel I thought. Feels the way vermin looks.

Also poorly built from an engineering standpoint. Which added to my disdain.

I wanted to smash it instinctively. In my blood I knew I wanted to standing right there on the side of the road as it chunked and clattered to wherever it is they go when they're off duty. I felt carbonated inside of myself. Bubbling over like a chemist's beaker. It stopped and looked at me and into me and through me and waved a tentative hello with its hinges and I waved back out of habit.

It said hey man how's it going.

Then I felt guilty about feeling all of that spite when the friendly ball-busting had subsided and my phone was quiet and it was just my brain texting itself back and forth in my bed that night.

Maybe we should just get used to them I thought. Their inevitability.

I have never killed anything before in my life. Aside from thousands of bugs which do not count obviously and dozens of caught fish which do not count obviously and the occasional roadkill which does not count obviously. Except maybe for the deer in Vermont but that one was a coin flip on which of us was going to go out. Standing there afterward in the wreckage and the blinding slush watching it hyperventilate itself into nothing.

I wouldn't have even known how to transform it into meat had I thought to think of that. I just left it there for something else to find.

There were also the thousands of chickens and cows someone else had killed on my behalf where the culpability in terms of that was negotiable.

I think I know what you're feeling one of my friends texted me the next day. It takes a while to get over that instinctual…and then the bubble sat there for a minute or more pulsing like a heartbeat. Like he was editing himself.

But you have to he said. You have to get over it.

And so I did.

I did so gradually then all at once.

How to live

We watched every snap of the game. Both of us. Me and you. Everyone else did too. The commercials for Jesus from an evil church and the commercials for an ongoing massacre by an evil country. We watched the whole thing which was itself a commercial for the entire concept of this evil country of our own. I was going to say it is our essence distilled but that implies something being made small and more potent which is the opposite of the Super Bowl and America neither of which can be diminished but instead can only expand.

Devour.

I don't know.

Something so garish defies metaphor. Something so large defies metaphor.

If a towering beast appeared on the horizon laying waste to everything in its path right now you wouldn't think to describe it as being like something else you would simply and dumbly perceive its horrible mass.

Unless that exact thing happened in a foreign movie in which case it would typically be a metaphor for America.

Hold on someone is at the door.

It was some guys delivering our new mattress. I asked them if they would help me carry it up the stairs and they said no. So now I have that burden.

There were pummeling civilians in a densely packed area of Gaza that people had previously been told to go to for safety. You could tell it was a bad one this time because even CNN was assigning agency to Israel in their reporting.

I had a brief notion that this tension I was feeling was something remarkable but it wasn't at all. It was just how every day is anyway for those of us lucky enough to live how we do.

A matter of course.

I scrolled by an image of a little baby Palestinian boy whose head looked like a smashed jar of tomato sauce and had to immediately avert my gaze. I thought that this has to happen for some reason. Every day this has to happen.

Even though I only half saw him I can still see him now like a bright red migraine aura when I close my eyes.

Then a picture of me and you came up in my phone memories from the Super Bowl years ago in Houston. The greatest comeback in history!

Look how happy we were. Like nothing else mattered.

I need to be distracted again like that. I need to be distracted from this. They should have the Super Bowl again tonight.

I'm just thinking out loud here.

Tomorrow too. Make the entire year out of Super Bowls. An entire country of it. Spreading and swelling. One game after the next. Script it like that. So that our easy lives may never be interrupted by new word from the world.

I don't think I know how to live correctly. If there is a correct way.

What does a person do?

The next morning it was a sunny February Monday in Massachusetts. I should have been hungover if I could still get hangovers. They were saying that we were supposed to be buried under a surprise foot of snow overnight. It was probably going to be a day off for the kids.

This is my blood

I marvel at the design of our weapons. So sophisticated that they can transform any man woman or child into a terrorist. Writing in their flight between launch and concussion an entire alternate history of a life.

Just as the cop's bullet convicts you of a crime. Its presence in your body evidence enough that it always belonged there.

A violent transubstantiation.

See the Moon 2

The famous eclipse from the newspaper and TV and phone was closing in hour by hour and all day I had been having this intrusive thought that I was going to stare directly at it raw even though I didn't actually want to do that for obvious health reasons. Like the little ghost that dances up your spine as the subway is pulling into the station.

About 30 minutes before curtain I walked out of the gym (which I go to by the way) and there were a number of people in the parking lot with the glasses on all looking up at the sky and so I did the most natural thing in the world the most obvious instinctive thing before catching myself at the last second.

Come on man.

I walked over to the grocery store staring straight down at the ground with every footfall like Charlie Brown at Christmas and a dragonfly landed on my shoulder.

The one from before. From the other book.

I emerged a grocery store's time later with two fistfuls of food bags and you can probably guess what happened again.

It wasn't yet spring but the puberty of spring and the pollen was beating the hell out of me. I had to sneeze so badly but it wouldn't take and there was only one thing I could think of to do.

I considered googling the most humiliating phrase I have ever thought of which is "how do you sneeze" but I knew I'd have to spelunk through five pages of ad chum and AI-generated bilge before I learned anything real so I just sucked it up and stood there not sneezing and inspecting the integrity of the pavement.

It all seemed to be in order.

I had been taking potions lately to be able to sleep and to shit which is shameful to me because those are two of the most famous things that mammals can do without even worrying about it. I didn't need to add sneezing to my ledger.

I glanced up about 45 degrees at the electrical poles draped with buzzing wires and noted the new absence of birds. The world felt like walking into what you thought was a dark empty house just before a surprise party explodes.

I turned the ignition in the car and turned the radio on in the car and they had reporters on talking about how it all looked in Mexico and then north and east up the path of totality city by city in a diagonal fashion and I'm sorry but radio seemed like an inefficient medium for this particular phenomenon. I listened anyway because anything is better than one single second of silence.

Of course a traffic jam pulling out of the shopping complex. Like before a blizzard. Everyone knew logically that it wasn't the end of the world but that would be what we would think right before the end of the world isn't it? Not registering it or accepting it.

Better to go out with a fridge full of milk than the alternative.

On the drive home I saw the guys at the machine shop standing outside in their welding helmets looking up at the sky and playing grabass. Delighted like little boys.

Like everyone else I had read Annie Dillard's essay Total Eclipse earlier.

"I turned back to the sun. It was going. The sun was going, and the world was wrong. The grasses were wrong; they were platinum. Their every detail of stem, head, and blade shone lightless and artificially distinct as an art photographer's platinum print. This color has never been seen on Earth. The hues were metallic; their finish was matte."

Powerful stuff to be sure it mostly made me think about another great piece of literature.

"The sky was gold, it was rose, I was taking sips of it through my nose and I wish I could get back there, someplace back there, in the place we used to start."

None of those words from either work of art applied to my situation here today as far as concerns the eclipse but it would have been pretty cool if they had.

I got an alert and I looked at it at the stop light at the fucked up intersection where I will be killed and die one day. It was my sister texting the family one of those filter image gags where it's supposed to show you what you're going to look like in twenty or thirty years and here she was as an old lady with the thin white hair and sagging skin and liver spots.

I texted you can't be thinking about that kind of thing yet my dear sister.

You have to just find out later I thought.

Some people are intrigued by the idea of knowing the exact day they will die but I don't even want to know what happens five minutes from now. It feels to me like reading the Wikipedia summary of a horror movie because you are too scared to sit through it.

Undignified.

On my block a neighbor was outside looking up at the sky and I said whatever you say to a person and she offered her eclipse glasses to me and I didn't really give a shit but also didn't want to be rude and so I took them and looked up and sure enough there was the whole thing almost happening. It was getting cold now and so I was getting cold and I stared for what I assumed would be long enough to be polite both to her and to the majesty of creation and then a couple seconds longer and said wow it looks like it's all coming together.

I am in possession of the exact sufficient amount of instinctual awe over the wonders of the universe that I am supposed to have. How small we all are etcetera. Meaningless in the grand scale of it all. But if I'm being honest and this is just between you and I it was all amounting to a kind of a jack off situation this eclipse. We weren't really getting the full thing here in this neck of the woods. More of a touring company production than the original Broadway cast.

Inside on the TV the news was bouncing around from city to city and interviewing people about how crazy it all was and I sat there for a while and watched people somewhere else watching the sky act weirder than usual and then outside of my window I noticed a bunch of other neighbors had gathered. They were standing together looking at you know what and I thought I had better go see what had developed celestially speaking.

There were some old folks from up the road who looked like my imaginary sister and a couple of young families and I said hey pretty cool huh to a few of the kids and I thought that they don't know what the world is yet. They don't know anything is bad yet.

Or worse maybe they do.

One of them said do you want to look and handed me her glasses and my Eclipse Grinch heart grew two sizes. She said they were kind of broken and I thought oh great I'm gonna go blind right here in front of everyone on the block just so some kid doesn't think I'm a pussy. I held them up to my eyes and everything went black until I could find what I was looking for and then... there it was. We all looked and looked and looked and I drank it in and drank it in and at long last it happened. It was like a miracle.

God bless you she said.

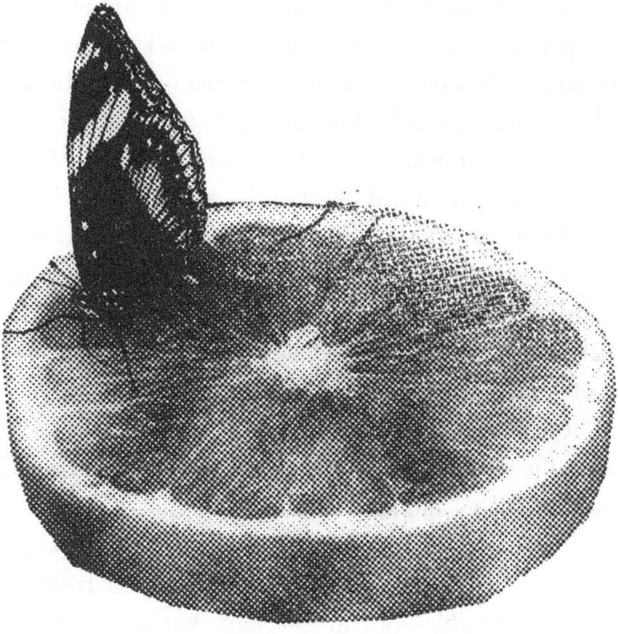

Something you are

Remind me what it is you said that you do again the dental hygienist said. I was laying back in the chair wearing the badass sunglasses they have you put on feeling like the Terminator getting repairs done and I said ohmma riattuh and she sniffed inside of her mask and said yes of course that's right. We haven't seen you in quite a while she said. She asked me to turn my head to the left and started scraping the sensitive part of my incisor with the implement and I winced and she said it's almost all over. I noticed her name tag dangling off of her lapel said Gray Maria. No comma. I understood the general gist of what it was meant to convey but got excited for a second about the coolest name I had ever heard. How are you holding on she said and then let me breathe and I said I'm fine in my normal voice. I used to be quite frightened of going to the dentist when I was young I said but now it's basically like whatever. I could pass out here I said. In a good way I mean. It was very scary when we were young she said. Were dentists back then really as cruel as we remember them or did you guys come up with new standards in bedside manner in the meantime I said. Or is it just to do with us being older and more comfortable with suffering I said and she said it's a little bit of both before going back to work on me. It was definitely worse back then though she said. No question about it. You couldn't get me to step foot in here when I was a kid she said. Now I'm here every day she said and I tried to laugh with my eyes. Then the dentist herself breezed in from backstage to give both of us a once over and told me I would need a crown sooner rather than later. This one is dying she said poking a gloved finger around my mouth. I thought of a fish on a hook. Prioritize fourteen she told the hygienist. Mark that down in his records she said. There will come a time when it's too late to be saved she said. She didn't even give me the hard sell on any other procedures and I couldn't decide if that made me respect her more or less. A TV screen on the wall in front of me was playing a video of a relaxing ocean tide on too short of a loop for it to have the intended effect. A jittery sea bird kept walking up to the edge of the water and hesitating in the face of it then disappearing off screen and coming back around again. This one needs another turn the hygienist told me. One more detail. Whaa gwahoo mahn I said. I thought of the smell of burnt hair and meat. I thought of a stampede toward the water. More tooth scraping now. I was acutely aware of the skeleton inside of me. When she let me close the bones of my jaw again I said I'm sorry if this is weird but is your name literally Gray Maria or is it Maria Gray and she laughed with her eyes and said no one has ever asked me that before. I was going to say that would have been a really cool name for a person to have I said. It's still a cool name either way I said and she said well you can use it in one of your little stories and I said that I would. Will she be good or evil she said. And what is it that the bird will want?

No living witness

Scrubbing dishes in a soup splattered sink. Rinsing out the plastic takeout containers before putting them in the recycling bin which I will later roll out to the curb like the most gullible man alive. To be able to tell myself that I had given it an honest try. You can lie to yourself about anything you want to if there's no one following up.

Jumbling and jostling and splashing like a child with a house hose and speak of the Devil out the kitchen window now appeared some actual children from next door darting around with a hose of their own on our shared grass. That's probably why I thought of the hose analogy in the first place just there.

Reminding me also I should get to cutting the grass.

Fine.

I will cut the grass tomorrow.

Do you ever hold the door open for someone at the grocery store or vice versa or perhaps someone waves to you to go through first in traffic and you want to weep for the world over it?

Everyone who has ever lived and died.

How kind we can all be to one another when it costs us nothing.

My tablet reading the news out loud saying they had found microplastics in the clouds in the mountains of eastern China and saying also that this was bad news because certain toxic metals like lead and mercury and other elements could cling to the plastic particles and be carried this way and that on the rain and wind to the places where it matters when things happen to people.

Describing it all in the same measured radio reporter tone and cadence that they might use to say something like terrorists are sneaking across the border. Which they also started saying explicitly in the next segment and is probably why I thought of the comparison.

That always seemed like such an Odyssean effort to me. When I hear them tell tale of these people supposedly traveling thousands of miles over air and sea and land with nothing and with no one just to come kill some random Americans on the other side of it.

And no hope whatsoever of it being one of our main guys. More likely it's the least powerful American you can gain access to.

I was going to say desperate people do not kill desperate people for no reason but that isn't really true. Most murderers I ever heard of just turn to the nearest weakest person available and get it over with and then regret it instantly.

Oh God what have I done?

Carrying on like that.

Then booted down into the hole. The ones we've built here and the much deeper ones we imagined into being for ourselves.

Forget about it though because that border story is not real so I do not have to think about it for one second longer. Never mind that Americans are fully eager to and capable of killing other Americans. No one can massacre one of us like one of us. Unlike most other dirty jobs we do not need to outsource that one to migrants.

Listen to me.

I do not want to waste my life on revenge.

I'm not particularly well read but I know nothing good comes from that in the books.

From what I understand digging a grave to dump a body into is famously hard work but it can be done with effort. Covering it back over is another thing entirely. A hole that can never be filled no matter how vigorously you shovel.

Now the kids are fighting one another. Worrying over who gets to control the water.

I thought just now of the copperhead snake we almost tripped over hiking in the woods by the lake. The noise we both made. And later what I thought was possibly a cougar standing just off to the side of the trail sizing us up. Calculating distance and velocity and force and mass. However felines measure the edible world.

You said later you were positive that it wasn't a cougar. There will be no doubt in your mind that you have seen a cougar if you ever see one you said. There will be no question at all.

Baby I want to live so badly.

And go on living without this pain or any kind of pain.

And I yearn for you not here right now drying these dishes as I pass them over to no one.

We have starved one another.

Our cheeks sunken in.

I hunger for you like the grinding garbage disposal asks for my hand.

No filter

I'm sorry to report that the apocalypse is going to look very cool for a little while before it fully kicks in. Not up close obviously. You wouldn't want that. I mean from the safety of a camera's framing. Debuting for us an entire new palette of prismatic skies with each disastrous iteration.

The smoke was bad enough this week that you had to contend with it no matter how far you lived from the nucleus. Plan around it. Never not be aware of it. Even career smokers going well this fucking blows. I can't breathe right and everything smells like shit. More so than usual.

Just because you're used to inhaling one type of smoke doesn't make you less susceptible to a second unrelated kind. How you might share a common language with someone but their accent is unintelligible. I'm embarrassed to say that I honestly kind of thought that it might and that one is on me.

This varietal was wafting in southerly with an aroma of peaty whisky which also paired very poorly with drinking an actual peaty whisky. You might think the flavor profiles would mingle well but you would be wrong.

I thought of a fly swimming for ten glorious final seconds in an unattended beer glass on a patio bar.

Come here though real quick dear. Look at this picture. It's a splintered electrical pole halved into an accidental crucifix. It's dangling from melting power lines in the very eye of a mountainous inferno. Almost as if it were hovering in mid air.

It looks like something out of real life.

You are in a museum

They drove up to Salem to be somewhere different for a little while. Anywhere different.

Salem was usually a magical place for them but not because of the whole mess every October. She could take or leave the Salem of it all so it was refreshing being there before the throngs of tourists who would be arriving shortly.

They naturally considered themselves the good kind of tourist.

The magic comes when you're not expecting it they both knew.

Stumble onto a random cobblestone street and there before you will stretch a block that you could convince yourself had remained unchanged for hundreds of years. That this is still what the world is. You might believe albeit briefly that you were standing there in 1700 and then you'd crumble into dust and blow away on the wind because the life expectancy back then was like 38. Which happened to be what they were.

This can happen sometimes in Boston too but so much more rarely now.

They walked around the main commercial area and it was bright and beautiful out when they turned left down a small street that the sun couldn't find and she swore to God that all of the leaves on the trees looked like they had just fallen moments ago and were resting dead on the ground. That the temperature had dropped twenty degrees right then and there in August.

Down at the end of the block there was a squat brick building that must have been a few hundred years old. She thought whatever had once gone on inside of there was none of her business.

Well this can't be normal she thought with the leaves crunching underfoot and so they turned heel and shortly thereafter all of that sense of foreboding was deflated while walking by about fifty different shops selling witch t-shirts and witch tchotchkes.

They got a lot of witch bullshit out already she said. I'm not sure what else I was expecting she said.

She thought about how awful it must have been living under the thumb of a draconian authority who ruled with suspicion and revenge as their entire animating principles.

Next walking into the Peabody Essex Museum. There was an exhibit of South Asian art about the effects of British occupation on Indian self representation and one on maritime art from around the world with a focus on Salem's seafaring history. He thought looking at all the paintings and objects more than anything that being on a boat any time before relatively recently in history must have fucking sucked. Getting violently sick and then probably drowning. All for some other guy's profit.

Pretty much sucks now too for that matter.

There had been a shooting recently so she felt on edge being in a crowded public space.

Seven members of a family in Ohio including a nine year old boy were shot in the head execution style. The shooter had become irate when the family asked him to stop firing off his AR-15 recreationally in his backyard so he killed most of them. Three of the other children survived. They were found covered in the blood of their mothers who were both killed while laying on top of them. Throwing their bodies in front of the bullets.

They safely hid a two month old under a pile of clothes.

Do you ever think about a shooting she asked.

By which she meant do you have a little pilot light of anxiety always burning somewhere inside. A little seed of dormant foreboding. Something strapped to your back like a heavy satchel.

I think about it more often in the aftermath of a bad one he said. I feel a bit more on edge in large public gatherings or in malls or wherever.

When do you ever go to the mall?

The proverbial mall. You know what I mean. But they happen so frequently now the reprieves in between don't last very long.

They were saying on my phone last night that you have to be prepared at all times like a soldier. Be prepared to kill anyone you see she said.

Fuck that he said. I refuse to think like that.

Sorry sorry he said speaking more quietly now. Remembering where he was.

I am aware of my surroundings he said. I don't take any unnecessary risks or instigate any stupid confrontations. But I will not give in to that way of thinking.

I look for exits more frequently now she said. It's just like looking both ways before I cross the street. It's automatic. I read someone say that somewhere. A habitual tensing.

They were quiet for a while after that and wandered into a large hangar-like room for what was supposed to be a show-stopper of a piece. It was called All the Flowers Are for Me and it was a giant floating cube of sorts constructed so the light from within reflected all over the walls in precise and ornate floral patterns.

It was the type of cube where you're not sure if it's going to impart some kind of ancient wisdom as you gaze into it or if it's going to absorb you into its horrible eternal gleaming she thought. Maybe both.

Mostly it was the kind of piece that people want to take Instagrams of which she did.

She shuddered suddenly thinking of three red throbbing pillars off the coast.

Moving on to an exhibit called Down to the Bone. Photographs of polar bears scavenging the remains of dead whales in an Inupiat village in Alaska. How tiny the giant bears looked climbing along the stripped-clean bones of the leviathans. She thought the skeletons seemed like they must have been arranged just so by the artist but then figured it's more likely they fell together like that in an accidentally beautiful deathly architecture.

"We have lots of bears here in Kaktovik because they have no place to go," a quote from a hunter read on the text card.

"The bears here are climate refugees. Soon we will be climate refugees too."

He stood looking on dumbly over her shoulder.

I don't know he said.

What?

I don't know if I'm any good at going to museums anymore. I try but I just don't really get uhh transported anywhere he said. Not like I do just standing on an old street. Like the one from earlier he said.

Which street she said.

I don't know.

He thought that museums necessarily strip away a few of our senses. Nothing smells like anything and you usually can't touch or thankfully taste anything so that just leaves the looking and sometimes the listening.

With so much quiet it's hard for me to block out the part of my brain that's operating in the background going you are in a museum.

You are in a museum and it is time to be moved by art.

They left soon after and rode an elevator up to a hotel rooftop bar that was just fine. Perfectly ok. Everyone seemed to be enjoying themselves drinking their frozen strawberry habanero margaritas and eating their roasted shrimp tacos with jack cheese and corn salsa and poblano crema.

At the bar the staff had a flyswatter out and they were using it to try to kill some bees that had found their way all the way up there.

I know this is probably stupid but it had never occurred to me that bees could fly up this high into the sky he said. I had always assumed they operated on a relatively low to the ground kind of deal. Occasionally flew up into a tree at the end of the work day.

I think this is probably about as high up as they can make it she said.

Five stories up he said. All the way into the sky and we're all acting like everything is normal?

It occurred to him that he didn't know anything about nature or the world at all. Who designed all of this shit? Who made it all just so he thought and then thwack they got one. Then another.

Thwack. Thwack. Thwack. Thwack.

The bartender was on a hitting streak now. The rest of the staff and all the day drinkers were cheering him on. He couldn't miss. He couldn't stop now if he wanted to.

The elevator dinged and someone was striding out of it now with purpose. They both turned on their stools. It was just some guy. It was no one at all.

**One of those dreams where you
fall in love with nobody**

I imagined you in the early morning. Invented you. One third awake. Half awake now. Dawning on me incrementally how I will shortly have betrayed both of us. Or what it will have always had to have been that you will have always had to have done to me.

Our coming shared loss.

The light through the chink in the armor of the cheap blinds that someone else had hung before I ever dreamed here.

Facedown and clenching the sheets like the napes of two cat necks.

An hour more.

Ten minutes.

Your perfect nose grew long and wooden then wafted in the wind as sawdust. Like in a movie about something.

Your eyes bleeding out in red ribbons

A quick detour where I'm being starved and tortured in a pig cage.

Then the scarlet mud of a missile smashed-in body.

Now the other dream where I'm dangling from a ledge before letting go and plummeting downwards into my waking world. The place I assume is real. And you falling into your own kind of jurisdictional oblivion in tandem.

But you know all of this as I alone have made you briefly exist and you live nowhere else but within me at least for these last waking counterfeit seconds.

Nowhere that I can find my way back to.

The cursed phone screaming.

The gallows' trap door.

This time I won't forget any of it. Our two cumulative hours together. When the full day's heat spreads out over everything plain and tangible I'll sit under my tree and hope that you too can see its branches reaching toward Heaven with your own eyes. With our eyes.

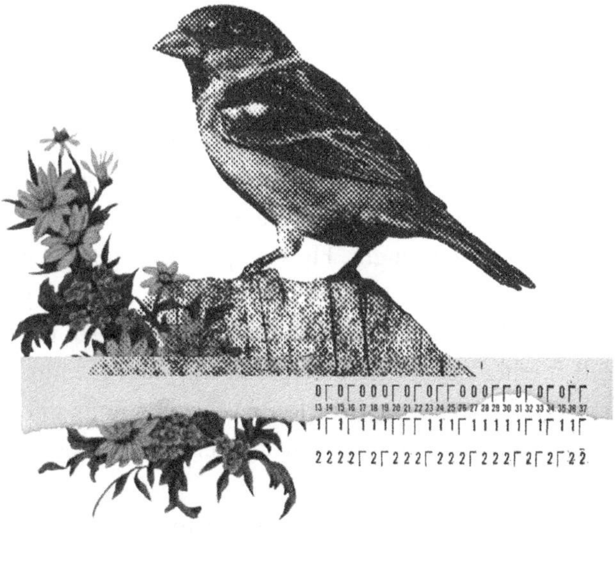

Such feasting

There are maggots all over the trash bag she said. Likely place for them to be he said but she didn't find that funny. They were spilling out of it all over the sidewalk. The bag must have been ripped open by the birds she said. He said fine and went out to inspect the scene of the crime. It looked like a swung sword had been slashed deep into a man's stomach and he had fallen to his knees. He said the line from Lost Boys and she thought that was a little bit funny and he went to get another bigger bag and the snow shovel to scoop the entire mess up into and gagged when he got near the wound. They were so much skinnier than he would have thought. How he pictured the concept of maggot. Not mature enough to have fattened yet perhaps. Infants. As he shoveled an avalanche of them fell further out of the gash in an off-putting kind of gravity. Like cheap animation. When you pour a beer too fast and the froth rises so suddenly and spills over the rim of the glass.

A man with a truck was going to arrive soon to take them on a trip to paradise. They had no idea how good they would very briefly have it. That they would soon be able to fly.

A hole in the wall

They slaughtered a score of kids and a mess of their teachers an hour from here. This was all supposed to be happening somewhere else. Somewhere we could fret about it sure but not be made to weep deeply over it. The kind of thing you give an afternoon of attention before forgetting.

An iceberg melting and collapsing into the water in Antarctica is one thing but now imagine it happening right there off the side of the highway on your commute to work.

It was an individual shooter not a plural they or a gendered they. But they did it nevertheless. All of them.

We despaired and so could think of nothing to do but post. To write something beautiful or angry. Both at once. Devastated but not defeated. Not fully defeated. Not even now. To reassert our collective humanity. To remind ourselves that this is all worth it somehow. All of this living.

A shortage of beauty of late as it happens. We've dug the beauty mines clean. The children we sent down into them to burrow haven't returned.

It was enough to make you want to get a gun.

Perhaps it would be better to post something profane. There's no shortage of ugliness to be found in this latest massacre.

Everyone we knew knew someone who knew someone.

I punched a hole in the goddamned wall. I've never done that.

Ok once during a football game I was watching.

It wasn't even that poorly received at home. The punching. How a family would normally look upon a father doing that. I thought briefly my wife might even punch a smaller hole of her own and then the kids too one by one. Each hole smaller than the previous one on down the line as per relative fist size. Having to hold the hand of the youngest to manage it.

Later after another shooting we could use the holes to measure how much bigger they had grown. Little pencil marks scribbled onto the crumbled plaster.

I should not have done that. I know that. But then again what should I have done?

Living in this place on a baseline violent day is already like taking part in a sick lottery. We wake up and spin the wheel and wait to find out later if we ourselves or someone we love will have our names read on the news. One of the roughly three hundred who are shot per day. One of the roughly one hundred who die.

But being well acquainted with a newly infamous school or mall or concert wrenches that grim gamble from a sort of abstraction into starkest reality. The moment when the wheel stops and the ball bounces into its slot.

A bullet makes such a small hole in a wall but such a large hole in a body.

I don't think agony is a strong enough word. I don't know if we have a word strong enough in the language to accurately convey how that would feel. There are sounds though.

I had a friend in college whose father was a funeral home director and he told me once he could never watch Law & Order or anything like that with him because the old man always got pissed off about how badly the actors conveyed the abominable cacophony of sudden grief.

Those aren't the noises people make he always said

People say we've become numb to this blizzard of killing but I don't feel numb right now do you? I'm still furious and horrified and for some reason I am taking a perverse solace in that. That I retain my capacity to feel anything at all. At least I have this anger and sadness. It's the thinnest gruel.

Not that anger or sadness seem to be mounting much of a defense against anything. What does grief do against a gun? Against this many guns. You might as well try putting out a fire with gasoline. Grief isn't the antidote to gun violence it's just the byproduct of it and a gun is a machine designed to spread as much grief around as quickly as possible. They're cancerously good at what they're made to do.

We all have our routines we repeat. Have our patter down. The Onion headline. Do our wry jokes cut with darkness. Cuss all of them out. Our little superstitious rituals. Like a baseball player at bat adjusting his gloves just so.

We get an awful lot of awful at bats.

There's a poem about this that we all share every time. Every other month. Well it's a lovely enough poem that one poem but who gives a shit? What does it change? What can a poem do? I'm afraid the poets are on a very bad losing streak. They're going to have to rewrite the record books.

I wrote that exact sentiment somewhere online after a previous massacre I believe. Whichever one. It doesn't matter. I'll post it again soon.

The father of one of the latest batch of dead little girls went on the TV. I don't know how he did that. How he could stand up never mind speak in sentences. He told us about his daughter. He said she always brushed her teeth. She was so young that that's what he was most recently proud of her for having learned to do. She had only made it as far as that developmental milestone.

She always brushed her teeth.

Sometimes I even forget to do that and I am however old I am.

This is stupid I know but I still kind of think it will never happen to us. My specific children. Even knowing what I know which is that there isn't a type of place where these things cannot and will not happen except almost every other country in the world.

Yet I still think that. What a weird thing to think. You kind of have to do so to function right?

I know I said I'm not numb a minute ago but you have to numb some parts of yourself or else who could ever get out of bed?

Here's something else ugly.

It's hard to pick just a few things to reflect on from this one but you can't comprehend all the ugliness at once. Instead you focus on one or two waves and they give you a general idea of the tide they came from.

The husband of one of the freshly dead teachers died of a heart attack the next day. You could maybe convince yourself there is something beautiful about that. Loving someone so much that losing them literally breaks your heart.

I'm not inclined to feel that way at the moment. That it had cause to happen in the first place is one of the ugliest things imaginable. I don't know what happened exactly but it's very easy to think of this guy sobbing so hard that his body gave in.

Maybe he had punched so many holes in the wall that his entire suddenly empty house had collapsed around him.

Metaphors are useless now I'm sorry.

He was murdered by them. All of them. The same killer using the same gun that killed his wife.

What an invention these guns are. One bullet toppling an entire family.

The efficiency of it.

They all must delight in this kind of thing. They plural. The gun people. I wonder if they see anything beautiful in a bullet's trajectory. How far they can fly. Killing people they weren't even aimed at.

Personal best

She was on the treadmill when all of the TVs at the gym switched to coverage of the attack. Even the ones that usually show commercials for Planet Fitness while you're at Planet Fitness. She'd never seen them do that kind of thing before.

Actually one down the end still had Pat McAfee and Aaron Rodgers on. Not even the imminent threat of a World War III will relieve us of these men.

And then she just kept running. Notched the speed and elevation up and glided off the surge of adrenaline that televised destruction brings. Ran like the fucking wind in fact. How thrilling death can be from a distance.

Besides there was no way they would ever get to us here she thought. The odds of it. There would be no point in trying to get to us here. So far from anything important. So far from anything real.

It was such a strange feeling but she figured that if it's meant to be the end of the world then she had better be in shape for it. Have that at least as a starting off point.

She ran for miles. She was going to outrun any of their missiles. She was a missile herself now.

Around 45 minutes in a guy hopped on the next treadmill over and started trying to get her attention. Motioning for her to take her headphones off.

The CVS down the street from me

I do not appreciate being treated like I'm a scumbag addict when I go to pick up a prescription at the pharmacy just because I look like one and also am one. Wrong kind I want to tell them. Different genre. There's nothing you have back there that could ever heal what is wrong with me. Not even temporarily. On the other hand they got those little pre-wrapped charcuterie joints I like for $9.75 in the fridge up front so it's not like it's all bad. ⅖ stars.

The Song You Wanted It to Be

See the ducks down there she said pointing like a child points. The black and white ones she said and he said where and she corrected herself and pointed again like an adult points and he said I guess so I can't really see without my glasses. Do you want me to go get them for you she said and he said no he said he could go get his glasses himself if it came to it.

They're bobbing under the water like penguins she said and he thought do penguins do that? Dawning on him now that penguins of course must have to dive down to eat fish or what else were they supposed to live off of. Certainly no insects swarming about in the Arctic or Antarctic or whichever one penguins live in. Like warmer birds have to go chasing around after. Not yet anyway.

Where do penguins live A___ said and she thought about it for a second and said the Antarctic and he thought that that honestly does not narrow things down for me.

Which one is that supposed to be again top of the map or bottom?

Look at the city her brother T___ said from the other end of the porch. Just look at it he said and so they did.

The sun was reflecting off the skyline over the water about fifty miles south and they all looked upon it and thought that it ranged from merely beautiful to evidence of the existence of God.

No one said the latter out loud.

All the way this far up and there was the city shining across the ocean. Like in a fairytale.

One of the old scary ones.

It was as if angels were melting human ants with a magnifying glass.

Biblically accurate angels.

They got one her niece said. Their niece said. Pointing like a child points. The black and white ducks were busy hauling what looked like a decent sized fish out of the water and now a bunch of unrelated seabirds who didn't even seem to be friends with these two protagonist ducks started bitching at each other over the one fish. Sort of a gang territory situation. Perhaps the ducks were supposed to have been paying a protection fee.

A___ wondered if different kinds of birds can understand or not when they garble and cry like that at each other. Is it like an English to French kind of deal between bird species relatively speaking where there are borrowed words or is it a human to dog and vice versa scenario?

Dog to dog you have to imagine it's all pretty rudimentary for them to sort their own business out but a bird sees so much more of the world. A bird has a passport with so many stamps.

The wind came screaming in off of the harbor and their local version of the sun was now on its way toward setting. T__ was gathering his daughter their niece up in a blanket and saying let's go take our picture baby walking out onto the bluff of giant rocks smoothed over and over much earlier by much higher and much less forgiving tides.

One wrong step on those rocks and you're fucked A__ thought.

Having a vision he didn't like. Quick lightning in his brain.

We take a picture once a year like this T__ said back to the porch and his sister let's call her S___ said yes yes I know that. We know that don't we dear?

That's right A__ said.

He had poisoned himself near to death the night before on this exact cushion on this exact couch on this exact porch and was throwing down big swallow-fulls of the exact same poison acting now as a temporary antidote.

I'm going to slip off of those rocks to my death he thought and she said this will all be over quickly don't worry.

The tide will come she thought.

I love this song T__ said walking back over now with the little girl into the speakers' blast radius and bracing themselves against the wind. It was the very specific song you want it to be. Your first dance in high school song or your wedding song. Whichever one of those kinds of songs you're thinking of that is what it was.

Their wedding song had been Us by Regina Spektor but they weren't listening to that one all that much anymore.

Are you cold A___ asked the girl his niece their niece and she struck a pose and said I'm not cold I'm cool and they all laughed like you do when a child tells a joke that's just ok.

Dinner next at a long wooden table that probably cost more than A___ makes in three months. Four adults two kids and one of them her nephew their nephew surfing on a chair. Going I'm Mr. Iron Man! Saying shit like that. Doing Goku punches at invisible enemies.

Can I have one of your chicken fingers A___ asked the boy and he said no with such rebuke. Like he'd been asked to donate a kidney tomorrow.

The kids' mother had just arrived today after being held up at work in the glowing city last night and so she was settling in like an old house settles and after a lull they turned to the details of her drive up. Everyone weighing in on the costs and benefits of fleeing at certain hours versus others.

Nothing much else to talk about besides things that were directly going unsaid.

There was this rabbit I saw that had been killed on the side of the road V___ said. She couldn't stop thinking about it she said. This particular rabbit had been fucking her up all day she said passing the butter for the lobster.

None of them before she arrived had really had a handle on how to kill the lobsters humanely. This always having been her duty. Deciding after all to just let them boil alive then step out of the room out of some kind of pantomime of reverence.

I'm Mr. Iron Man and I can fly!

A___ had said an Our Father to himself just in case while torturing the lobsters and felt stupid about it.

What about the rabbit bothered you so much S___ asked her sister in law and she said it was just laying there crushed to a pulp. Dirty.

Isn't roadkill pretty common on that stretch A___ said and she said yes yes it's just that it was all the way seven lanes across the eight lane highway. It must have been running from the woods on the southbound side toward the water.

What do you mean he said.

Well it almost made it.

Tomorrow now today and A___ and S___ on Good Harbor beach watching a tiny piping plover hobbling weirdly in the sand in the opposite direction of some ladybugs it must have been hunting for poorly.

They eat the ladybugs you would think A___ said.

The sky bright then reddening. Blushing.

The two of them loomed over the strawberry insect like pre-mourners at a terminal patient's bed as it inched and trudged hauling some kind of tiny burden or prize. Like hunters over game you've just shot and isn't dead yet.

What is that it's carrying A___ said and she said sand. It's carrying sand.

Why sand he said.

Why anything she said.

To fortify things maybe she thought. Its version of the world.

I'm going to walk right out into the water she thought and he didn't say anything about that. Pretended he hadn't known about it.

Why carry the sand from here to there he thought to say and then said a different stupider thing.

It's everywhere. This sand.

It really is baby she said. It's everywhere she said. That's what the beach is she said losing interest in that particular thread then squatting around until she harvested three shells with what she envisioned as tiny perfect little necklace holes. Shells the kind of purple that only occurs near the shore. One for each of the girls at the house she thought.

He tried to light a cigarette with some difficulty considering the aforementioned wind and smoked it briefly and sourly and sort of counterfeit like an actor smokes a fake cigarette on TV before crushing it out after two fake drags.

No one can pretend to smoke right. Not even actors whose main activities include pretending and smoking in between the pretending.

He thought of a crab coming along later and picking up the cigarette. How everything accidentally human an animal does is funny.

Everything animal a human does much less so.

He expected her to tell him to pick up the butt and transport it across the sand back to the trash cans at the still-April-shuttered guest center but she must not have been paying attention. He felt like he was getting away with something. But such low stakes.

She was watching a seabird with something in its mouth flying some distance off the coast into the wind and having a hell of a time at it and she thought you idiot just turn around. What is it that you need to get to uphill so urgently?

Look at what we allow

They said he threw his jacket. Kept saying that over and over. The man was agitated on the subway and he threw his jacket. I don't know what that means. I understand the basic physics of the action being described mind you and I understand why they would immediately start printing something like that in the newspapers because I guess in theory it suggests aggression that begged for a response. Not the one it got but still.

He threw his jacket they said. Kept saying. I don't know what that means.

Try throwing a jacket right now. What have you done? Nothing. Tom Brady could not throw a jacket especially hard. You couldn't hurt a person by throwing a jacket. You couldn't even hurt a small animal. Throwing your jacket on top of one is what you would do to specifically not hurt a bird that has gotten into your house. So you could carry it gently back outside. So that it could go on living.

The man's killer was a marine which triggered the media to use the same exonerative tense that they always use for cops. The most lethal among us always also the most blameless.

How people make excuses for certain breeds of dogs.

That hierarchical framing shows up a lot in bicyclist vs. driver stories and in the common use of homeowner as an honorific in a crime story and most especially in any normal citizen vs. homeless person story which is what this was.

Not just one specific group of normal citizens vs. one specific homeless person but all of them vs. all of them.

And it's a Thursday in May and a man is dead. Do you feel any safer?

I guess this one isn't fiction. You and I are just talking here.

I told you before that I know it can be uncomfortable to encounter an unhoused person in distress but that is because it is an up close and personal look at How It Actually Is. A peek under the hood of this country. The churning gears and foul combustion. It's no wonder then that so many of us want these humans simply disappeared. And they are humans in case you need reminding.

They aren't a threat so much as they are an indictment.

Look at what we allow.

It's the hideous beating of the tell-tale heart.

Much like with the existence of any billionaire the inverse here is that so many systemic mechanisms that should have been in operation had to have failed for any individual unhoused person to exist in the first place. It's shameful to see and so of course we all feel uneasy about it.

It's not so much seeing how the sausage is made it's seeing the sausage after it's been digested.

You told me about something you learned in school. A professor said that one of the things that helped people accept their work as concentration camp guards was that the terrible conditions of the camps themselves made the prisoners' literal filth synonymous with their inherent filthiness. If they weren't dirty then they wouldn't be this dirty.

It applies to modern prison guards and the ICE kidnappers as well. Look at this worm living in the wormhole. Writhing in its own muck.

Doing it to offend my sense of decency come to think of it. A personal insult to me.

Will no one rid me of these insects?

Let me ask you something. Take a quick inventory of your life. Like mine it's currently a mostly comfortable and safe one right? But be honest with yourself. Do you feel closer to the chasm of poverty with perhaps a devastating medical bill or an eviction or a ruinous encounter with the police or a worsening struggle with addiction or closer to the attainment of wealth and power?

Which end of the see-saw are you actually sitting on?

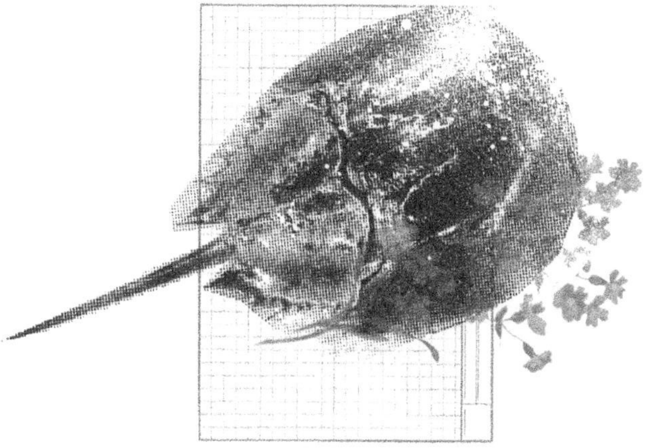

I had been being so good

I had been being so good. Everyone talked about that. How good I had been being. They got me by the balls soon enough though. I got myself by my own balls. You can picture what I'm saying. Turns out my organs are bad. Liver being the headliner. Not working right anymore the guy said. In terms of functioning. Filtering out certain chemicals and toxins and the rest. Whatever else they told me it does. Put it down to all of that business with the whisky. My ex-doctor told me this was coming up the pipe sooner or later years ago. My ex-wife too. I told them both to kiss my ass. Not literally but in so many words you know? Wives and doctors know you better than you know yourself. Have certain data that you do not have access to. Can't be bothered to read rather. I never really believed that later was an actual place I'd ever have to live in. Later was the goddamn moon. Something to contemplate in the dark and then avert your eyes. Frankly I had been counting on them having sorted this whole pickle out by the time it mattered for real people i.e. me. Then the thing with the scientific funding and the takeover of the universities. When I was a child I thought we were well on our way to flying cars someday so this was just another in a series of bad predictions on my part. Did George Jetson or any of those guys drink scotch now that I think of it? Maybe press a button and it comes out of a little chute on the wall. Some robot bartender being a wiseass. I do not remember correctly. I know they had that one bar in Star Wars. I don't remember so many things anymore. For already stated reasons. I don't even remember why I needed poisoning this badly to begin with. I never wanted to die I promise you. I always wished to live an average life I just needed some other surrogate guy to do the bulk of it on my behalf. Then pass the baton of my soul back off to me when it was my turn to sprint the final lap. When I was a Boy Scout they used to tell us the number one thing was to leave the campsite better than it was when you found it. So that it looked like no one had ever even been there.

The point of all of this

The most illiterate fascists alive were gassing themselves up because the computer had gotten some small degree better at producing dog shit that had the general production values of a circa 2004 video game cutscene. Delighting in the approach of a spiritually and culturally dead future devoid of art and meaning.

You do have to admit that a new Narcos season starring Brad Pitt and Mr. Beast and Jason Kelce sounds pretty sick though.

There's only one flaw I can see in this supposed AI-generated future of seven fingered bikini babes with death behind their eyes and photorealistic Family Guy pornos: I don't understand where they think their personalized sense of aesthetics they plan to input into the computer is going to come from down the line when all human artists have been driven out of business. If you want something perfectly tailored 1:1 to your own taste meant solely for you to experience alone you can already do that just by sitting there and thinking about it buddy. Skip the middleman step of the computer. It's just going to put it back in your brain anyway.

It's like puking food up just to eat it again.

Imagine a dog.

Fewer paws than that. A real dog.

Like my books or don't not my problem but I cannot tell you how many hours every day for a year or more I spend for example moving the word "that" around in a sentence over and over again trying to land the perfect percussion of it. Is this inefficient? Yes! It is also the whole point of it.

The drums have to be tuned

This probably applies to all of you. People in possession of human souls who have at least on occasion felt the divine in a work of art. Everything I write myself and everything I love to read or listen to or watch has one bedrock component to it which is this:

Jesus Christ I am alive right now and you are alive right now and someday we will not be but for the duration of this we are both stupidly and beautifully alive.

Please bear witness to my humanity and take some small portion of it for yourself. Return the favor to someone else later when you can.

I have a hangover again

I would prefer to be ushered hospitably and gently back into the world each morning more frequently than I have been. A warm welcome for a valued guest from the gal at the front desk and the kindly groundskeeper tipping his hat in the sun. Instead being hauled out of the driver side window of the bed and tossed onto the smashed glass by the constables who govern my awakenings. Even these imaginary ones corrupt and abusive. Locking me right back into the jail cell I was already inside of.

The eventual truth

We were going to have to put Jodie Foster down. I told my son we were sending her to the very same farm upstate my parents had conjured for me the last time this scenario played out when I was a child.

Massachusetts doesn't even have an upstate. That should have been my first sign something was amiss back then. But a child's brain cannot accept the concept of death. That differs from how an adult might think about it constantly and still not accept it.

She hadn't been hungry much of late but I kept smuggling pieces of my dinner into her bowl when no one else was looking anyhow. Hoping that a switch would flip in her tiny brain.

She knew something was weird about it and I knew that she knew that.

I got the idea that she instinctively sensed that I was bullshitting her somehow. Dogs are so dumb but an old dying dog is wise enough. Knows things we do not.

She looked at me like I was the one with the problem. Maybe I smelled different. Maybe a person smells just off in a way that we cannot perceive ourselves when we're devising a betrayal.

Or is it that what I was steeling myself to do now was the inverse of that?

Does loyalty smell like anything?

Grief affects all of us differently. I just accidentally wrote ad copy for a sneaker campaign there for example.

She limped the sideways way she walks now over to me after having not eaten any of the slop of meat sauce I'd purloined for her earlier and put her dog head on my human knee and I looked into her dog eyes and asked her what if it turned out that the farm is actually real somewhere honey? Why not? Why wouldn't any single thing we wanted to be real be real for just this one time?

An occasional gesture of benefaction that I believe that we are owed.

An extra hour of rec time for the prisoners.

She didn't react to that.

But then in that case which of my dead friends would I play with first when I visited the farm some day I worried. Which of them was the actual best girl in the whole wide world?

I told the boy about a time before he was born when I caught Jodie Foster lumbering home from the neighbor's yard with a rat half in her mouth and her snout caught in a trap the rat had also been caught in. Proud and ashamed at once like a bronze medalist. She would have eaten anything back then I swear to you.

He asked if we would ever get to see her again and I told him the only thing I know to be true.

Moon blindness

They were shooting poems into space. Tucking them into cozy little capsules inside of the rockets. This latest batch was supposed to head toward Jupiter's moon Europa and then Saturn's moon Titan they said.

Perhaps it was inevitable that our poets would grow tired of our own antiquated moon. They had long since stripped it clean of metaphor.

Can you imagine what poetry must be like on one of those science fiction planets where they have multiple moons? Or some kind of distinctive moon with more personality than ours?

I can't think of any space films where they focus on all that much poetry going on though. Everyone usually too busy shooting lasers and running from dinosaurs.

Perhaps they just never get around to showing us that pocket of space life and there is always poetry being scribbled about the tidal waves of diamond sand and the stabbing shores of acidic oceans and purple carnivorous canopies and floating rock formations just off camera in every single world any of us has ever envisioned.

Then again it's possible more moons is actually worse from a poet's perspective. You have to allow for that.

Stasis amidst abundance of choice.

Could be that the relative scarcity of moon for us is what animates the soul so to speak.

No one had made it clear why they were doing this stunt in the first place. In the hopes that someone somewhere might find them much later on and have to contend with this untranslatable mess concerning what our most educated alcoholics were so morose about all the time?

What we thought birds symbolized.

All of the different names of trees we had come up with.

The shapes of the shadows cast on the walls after divorce.

Whether war is good or not.

Either way it all seemed like a lot of trouble to go to for poems that no one was ever going to read. Not in a thousand years. They could have just published them the old fashioned way down here in a book.

Withdrawal

He had rehearsed a whole closing argument all morning. Preparing like a lawyer on a TV show would. How he imagined they would. Bulleting the facts of the case in his favor. Beat by beat. Memorized even the pauses. Was off book by lunch.

He wasn't a lawyer on a TV show as it so happened he was a lawyer in real life. A bad one too. Some fucking guy. Some sweating asshole.

But I love you he told her.

Tossing out all of his notes now.

I love you in italics.

As if it were the smoking gun itself. The bloody knife. And it was in its way but with an improper chain of custody.

I love you.

Saying it in this crackling falsetto unfamiliar to both of them.

God how embarrassing. To feel anything yes but more than that to feel things so basely. A dog standing there in pants.

Looking around to see if the neighbors could hear them talking. He felt all of a sudden as if he'd just been caught reciting the Pledge of Allegiance in the shower.

If someone besides God could hear what he thinks at 4 am when they are negotiating.

The landlady probably sitting inside the first floor of the triple decker peeking out from behind the lace curtains and frowning into her tea.

A landlady is one kind of a God.

She never liked him he knew that and he guessed she was right not to. Her husband dead coming up on these twenty five years now she often told them when she struggled up the steep back hallway steps with fresh baked Armenian Easter bread.

Saying it neutrally every time. Just a biographical fact. Like you'd tell someone what your job is. Or an addict saying how many years they had.

He whimpered that he loved her right there on the sidewalk in front of his suddenly haunted and cold apartment and she said I know you feel that way and the flowers he was holding slide-whistle wilted like in a cartoon.

He wasn't really holding flowers but he should have been. He had meant to get some flowers earlier so that counted as a thought. You can't tell her something like that though after the fact. Making excuses. You can't testify against yourself.

Just then the goddamned speeding ice cream truck pulled around the corner onto the block and hauled ass right by them. Not stopping either for a gaggle of neighborhood kids up the way trying desperately to wave him down. Like castaways when they spot a boat in the distance.

Not tooting his ice cream horn either. Not even that most baseline sign of respect.

He thought maybe and being generous here that it could be a surge pricing situation for the ice cream truck man. That there were children across town willing to pay more for their treats. Maybe the poor bastard was delinquent on the loan for his ice cream truck for all anybody knew and then he wasn't so mad at him for almost killing everyone every other day. Ferrying his wares from here to there and back again in a loop.

A big inhale.

Standing there in the world again.

I know that you believe that you… she said and trailed off and he noticed Kevin from next door fucking around with his truck. Just opening and closing the tailgate over and over it seemed like. Or mowing a patch of lawn that he already had mowed. Teaching the grass a lesson.

You see the Bruins last night Kevin shouted over and now he had to react to that. Masculinity tugging.

Fucking Pasta man he shouted back. Gambling that he had done something good or bad.

Brutal Kevin said.

Brutal he said.

She started once more:

I know that you believe that you…

She was eliding over the word love like it was a dangerous spell. How you can't say certain words in the mirror too many times. How you can't say the name of ___.

Or like the concept of love was a deep and endless hole burrowed into the earth's core. The lava down there belching and gurgling and what not. Minding her footing carefully and standing away from the infernal edge.

I know that you feel that way about me she said starting over one more time. But it's just a chemical reaction going on in your brain she said. Having brought in her own forensic science experts to testify.

She looked so beautiful he wanted to denounce himself right there in the middle of it all. Make a whole scene.

I did it! I did it you bastards! Drag me off to jail! God damn you all!

They'd have to call over the bailiff.

It's just a pair bonding thing she said. Like a habit kind of thing she said. There's a hormone called oxytocin she said and he said do you mean oxycontin which in retrospect he realized he should not have said.

He figured at the very least he could probably come to some kind of epiphany here. Gain some sort of awareness of who he was as a person. Learn from all of this and do better on the next iteration.

He wasn't going to do any of that. He knew that he could if he wanted to though. The door toward that path had been opened for him.

Then again there was always the chasm to fall into. The beckoning chasm.

Does lava kill you instantly or what? What's going on with lava lately? Kills fairly quickly you'd have to think. But how quickly exactly? How much suffering is involved? Sinking into it going ah fuck no fuck no.

He was thinking a child's thoughts to deflect from reality.

No it's a hormone from... I sent you an article about this she said and now he was screwed even worse. You have to read the articles girls send you.

When people have sex it floods their brains with a sense of affection and social bonding she said. Almost touching his face as a natural instinct but thinking better of it and trying to play it off as if she was just stretching weird. Now he was thinking about sex. It happens when people give birth too she said. Now he wasn't interested in sex. It makes mothers want to protect their children and immediately feed them. Now he was sort of half thinking about sex. On the fence about the entire operation.

So you're saying my mother doesn't love me either he said. Sort of as a joke but also to cynically introduce his mother as a defense witness here. She took him seriously and said you know that's not what I mean. Your mother has nothing to do with us. All of what that was with your mother...

Regarding the matter of his mother's love it was in fact up for debate but now probably wasn't the time to poke at that.

Then not knowing anything better to do in that pocket of time where each spoken sentence was a struck gavel he made everything worse by looking down at his phone. A nervous tic.

What are you doing she said and he showed her the video he had been watching when he was waiting for her earlier. It was some cops who had been sent to chuck homeless people's tents into a garbage truck in Arizona maybe. Somewhere like that. Somewhere made up.

They had stopped suddenly in their dirty labor and were now standing there in the video silently and at attention in the middle of the road while the Star Spangled Banner played somewhere off in the distance.

Standing solemn like. As if under a spell.

This is part of what I've been talking about she said.

I'm sorry he said.

I love you he said and she said yes but that doesn't matter. That does not matter at all because I am Adolf Hitler from the Nazis.

She didn't say that but that is how she looked saying it. How if Hitler was dumping you. How that would look.

I don't think that is good just so you know she said. What the police are doing to those people. In your video.

I know you don't he said and then the speeding ice cream truck ripped back around onto the block from the other direction. He figured the guy must have forgotten something at home. He slowed down a bit this time. It looked like he was giving him the finger as he drove by. Or possibly waving goodbye.

He hoped more than anything he would turn the music on. Please play the song he thought. Despite all of our differences man. That is all in the past now. Just this one time for me please. Play the little ice cream tune. For her more than me honestly. A little something to hope for. For the kids.

A fleeting thought that he could try to kill himself later as a last ditch escape but the problem there was that he didn't want to die so that complicated things. And if he made a big thing about it he'd probably have to go to the hospital and everyone would be pissed off after the initial concern had been sanded down.

No he wasn't going to do anything stupid like that. He was going to live. He was going to live unfortunately. To unfortunately live. And now with one more addiction to contend with. One he wasn't even aware that he had been suffering from this whole time. That we all are.

The last time we had dinner together

Someone in the cafe had burned a tray of croissants and the buttered smoke was suffocating so we thought twice about staying. Then they were scrambling around and eventually chair-propping open the door that had a sign on it explicitly instructing people not to do that very thing. We reasoned that we were in good hands in terms of ventilation and problem solving in the face of petty authority.

I sat down at the tiny little table with the tiny little sprig of something jutting out of the tiny little vase that places like this always have and almost immediately knocked it all over onto the people next to me seated there talking about I don't know let's say murder podcasts. Whatever it is people talk about now. M. went to wait in line to order and I pulled out my phone to help the short few minutes in limbo pass without having to confront a single moment of raw reflection. My bank had texted me again to say my account had been compromised but it was spam I am fairly sure. I hope that doesn't ever actually happen because how would I believe them at this point?

Next I saw a video of a storm in some windy wet city in which a car was pulling up to an intersection and it braked when a tiny little twister passed perpendicularly in front of it as politely as you please. The dangling traffic light barely swaying in its wake. As soon as it had made its way the car accelerated and drove on like nothing about it was strange like it was just some kids crossing to go to school. I wondered how long it will be before they have wind funnels on the driving map like they do speed traps and construction and I thought if that scenario had happened where I was from people would be beeping and cursing at it to get the fuck out of the road. Jumping out of the car to fist fight a tornado.

Then on my phone I saw some people arguing about student loan debt forgiveness and how it would only benefit the purple-haired baristas the most powerful political bloc in the country and I looked up and watched M. asking a few questions of the worker at the counter and had like a Leo pointing at the TV screen moment in my head. Some people were just talking about you I thought to say. I had this brief hallucination where I went up and wrote in a $10,000 tip on the bill and how ecstatic the barista would be to get it and there's me smiling and telling everyone instantly what I did and feeling like the world's singular philanthropist then like ten minutes later going I'm ruined I'm fucking ruined. Why did I do that? Going back to bargain with them to please accept $100 instead. I'm just some guy. I'm sorry. I made the mistake of generosity.

Here was my coffee and unburnt croissant now. M. was looking out the window behind me so I turned around and there was a striking white brick building that could have been 50 or 300 years old for all I knew with a giant mural-like splash of ivy diagonally across it that looked like a Phoenix exploding onto the horizon. M. said look at that it's like a painting and I did look and it was like a painting. I told her I agreed that it was like that. Next door to it was an old red brick school house type building with its own greenery growing upward but in this instance looking more like swaying vegetation at the bottom of the ocean reaching to entangle lost sailors. I glanced up to the roof to check for sirens. I wanted to take a picture of both buildings to show everyone so badly for some reason. I don't know why this type of contrast of nature and habitat appeals to our collective estimation of architectural beauty although it basically explains the entire aesthetic of fancy colleges. You would think it would be the opposite of beautiful considering how we really do not want vegetation and its attendant wildlife to encroach into our homes but could be we want to toe the line where inside meets out in terms of beauty's threshold. You certainly wouldn't like ivy or any other kind of plant grasping inside of your house. You'd pay a lot of money to prevent that.

Some moth larvae had infested our closets recently and it drove M. mad in the process as she selected each garment of ours one by one and inspected it with her Terminator scan until it was determined everything made of cloth in the entire upstairs needed to be sterilized.

What is it about unborn insect babies that repulses us more than the mature version? Like if you saw a couple spiders in your bedroom you'd go ah there's a couple spiders but if it were spider eggs that's something much worse. Maybe it's to do with the fear of the unknown or the hypothetical always being more alarming than the established present.

I wasn't quite as bothered by the whole moth thing in this case. I figured at worst I'd take a pair of pants out of the drawer one day down the line and some moths would have eaten the dick out of the crotch in big cartoon holes and I'd be like you got me there. Respecting the gag.

I couldn't stay to help for too long with the delousing because I had planned this big but entirely unremarkable thing with my parents and sisters where we would have Sunday dinner. Just to have a dinner. My parents and sisters and me alone. The five of us and nothing else. No tricks or occasions or anything. Just to sit in the house we used to all have dinner together in and do that. I could not and cannot now remember the last time that happened and as it turns out no one else could either although we certainly tried.

I had sort of become enamored with this idea that there was one day we all got together at the table and ate like a family and it was the last time that it happened and none of us knew it was happening and barely registered it as anything at all.

Endings are easier to suffer through when you aren't aware they're transpiring.

I know it probably seems like nothing to have dinner with your family but it is not nothing in our case. I can't think of the last time I ate a meal prepared for me by my mother outside of a holiday type of situation which is different for reasons I can't quite articulate.

I worried on the drive down that I might be forcing something here with this little stunt of nostalgic domesticity but it ended up being exactly what I wanted it to be. It's not like I don't want their children or our spouses around by the way but it's a different thing if you understand me when your overlapping familial identities are fractured. One can't fully be a sister when one is also being a mother and on down the line.

My mother took out old photo books and made us take home ones that each of us were featured in most prominently like she was dealing cards and we laughed and said remember this and remember that and said oh my god look how fat or not fat I was in this one and asked who is this person and who is that person and sometimes they had died in the meantime and sometimes we couldn't even remember their names or much about them at all which is a kind of dying.

Then we had prime rib and it was quite rare and my mother was worried it might be too rare and I told her it was not and meant it. Tom Brady was losing and me and my dad had that to talk about while the last in a long line of a family golden retrievers begged at my heel although begging doesn't describe it more like pushing its snout into my space like a commuter shoving onto a packed subway car. I fed it a few scraps of fat off the beast on my plate and then thought to ask after if it was ok to do that and when they said yes but just a little I gave it a few more scraps and the dog nuzzled my knee and it was the perfect trade me having nothing to offer this dog but gristle and the dog having nothing to offer me but affection and so we were square in that transaction.

Our cousin was in remission so we were happy about that although our uncle was declining into the bad phase of his Parkinson's and I mourn for him because it is how his father died and that wasn't pretty. I thought of a photo I saw in the earlier memory shuffling aspect of all of this where the old man was standing so straight and stoic next to a giant horse that I am sort of just learning that they all had at one point.

I was in the cafe again watching a video of a bull jogging along the side of the highway in what looked like Wyoming or somewhere like that. It had uprooted this entire wooden circular fence enclosure someone must have worked pretty hard on to keep it inside of. Maybe not hard enough actually. Spitting in that guy's face with every step and barely even having its stride hamstrung by the weight of the resistance. Just ahead of it up the way another wholly unencumbered cow was looking back like come on buddy keep up. Judging her friend like. No idea how impressive a feat it was to be able to carry on like that.

Now I was back at my parents' house. I proposed this dinner of just the five of us a few months ago and everyone instantly thought I was doing it as a pretense to come tell them I was dying or was going to kill myself which ok fair that's not out of the realm of possibility for what a person who knows me would think I might do but it's certainly out of the realm of possibility of things I would actually do. Still I told my mom when I walked in I had cancer which wasn't funny but she laughed after a few seconds then punched me in the stomach.

I would honestly declare it instantly if I were dying. To my family and to all of you I would go I have cancer lol. Or whatever it is I'm going to end up having. That is as far as I've planned out ahead as everything that comes after seems like it sucks too bad to imagine.

When I left we all posed for a picture and looked at it and said oh my god I look so fat or old etc and we all said this shouldn't be the last time we ever have dinner together like this but it probably will be. At least now we'll know the exact date.

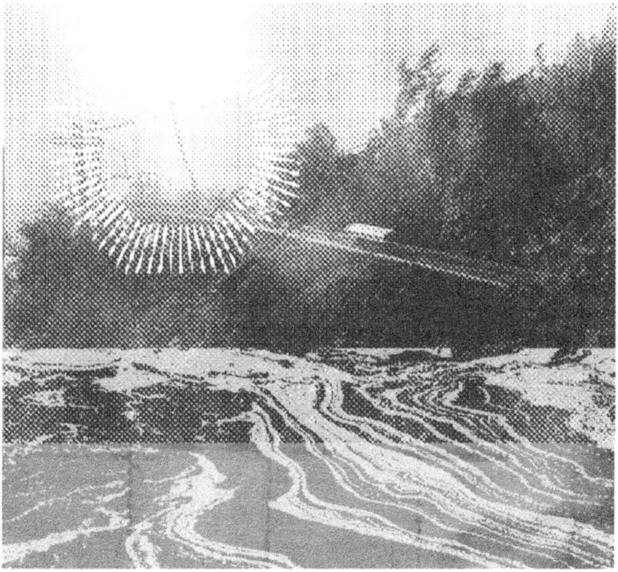

Boston, Massachusetts

We were back in the city for the first time in a good while and not recognizing many of the new businesses or even the skyline itself a melancholy overrode the initial excitement of it. The criteria for my melancholy are not especially rigorous to state the obvious.

I mentioned it to some friends later and we talked a bit about nostalgia for our youth and the pain of that but it wasn't quite getting it right. I'm not pining for something that is unattainable like the past I'm frustrated by not having access to something that still exists which is the city. It's all still right there just without me inside of it.

I thought of the old Bobcat Goldthwait joke:

I lost my job. Well I didn't lose it. I know where it is. There's just some other guy doing it now.

The next day we walked around our perfectly nice suburban town and it was perfectly nice. I stopped to take a picture of a fire hydrant that's in the process of being swallowed up by the overgrowth of brush on a quiet street by the river and thought of the end of the world. The criteria for me thinking about the end of the world are also not especially rigorous.

It's not the same of course. Out here. Nowhere. It does not nourish me in the way the city does. Did.

I need to be around people. Strangers.

I long for the camaraderie of our shared indifference to one another.

I wish for no one to care that I even exist.

The community in that.

How many human bodies

I own one single tree on the fraction of one single acre I also own the dirt and bugs of and it's so stupid to me that that's legally true under the laws of man who are responsible for regulating the laws of God when he's not looking.

Look at this magnificent wooden phoenix soaring here two hundred feet high unfurling its wings closer and closer to the clouds infinitesimally every second.

I wake up and go outside on a pigsty humid or arresting frigid morning and stretch up and out and inhale so big when the air is still amenable to it and look over at this tree doing the same move but that's where the similarities end between us. It must be three hundred years old this creature and so everything and everyone that was around when it crowned out of the earth is dead and gone by now and a lot of it all absorbed into its growing. How many exhaling human and animal bodies aided in its girth?

Right now two squirrels are chasing each other around its bark and bulk spiraling up and down running without gravity like two Spider-Men. Spiders-Men. They're undulating their tails in a way I've never noticed before in this hypnotic movement. Undulating is a gross word but it is accurate. I kind of get how it would fire them up to be honest. It's not like we don't do stupider dances to get laid.

We had some workers come over and cut off a couple of the tree's arms so they wouldn't break into our house and I'm sorry about that if anyone is listening who can absolve me for that sin. As I mentioned God isn't available.

I can't believe I own this tree. I have to go talk to a lawyer who knows about property rights. Maybe better to talk to a philosopher. A druid. It's not right it should be the other way around.

On the other hand the tree doesn't even know that I exist and I'll be dead long before it is felled so who is the landlord here after all.

I suppose I could murder it. I couldn't personally my hands are too soft and my back is no good but I could pay those guys from before to do it. Formidable guys. To teach it a lesson about its incessant striving toward the beyond.

I sometimes imagine it indifferently watching or rather not watching me grow old. Throwing its dead leaves at me that I have to rake up year after year. Like how you treat a hotel room someone else will later clean.

And then I die so quickly from its point of view. I go so quickly. Like a dog's life. Like a squirrel's life. Chasing a girl around a tree one summer with nothing to live for but the yearning.

Then after that without anything else to leave behind besides this husk for something else to grow on top of. Could be an even bigger tree. The biggest one you've ever seen. And I'm in there somewhere with all of you.

The closet

He was feeling around for the nest in the back of the closet and there it was just where his daughter had been saying it was supposed to have been all week. A certain amount of guilt came over him with that realization. That he hadn't believed her. Worse he had lectured her on the unlikelihood. Well I've gotta take the L on this one baby he said which embarrassed her. A man his age talking like that.

He couldn't afford a team to come haul it out to be burned in the pits considering what they were charging these days and the business with the robots so the only other thing he could think of to do was to fist wrist deep into the paper pulpy combs of it to show her that it wasn't so scary after all.

A friend of mine had had one of these whole deals in his apartment not long ago he told her. Before you were born he said. Look at this he said. Just a handful of bites he said. Showing her his purpling arm. Should clear up in a few days he said. If anything it kind of feels good.

Nothing to lose sleep over anyway.

Daddy is still alive he said. And he always will be.

Here come try it yourself.

Jesus fucking Christ

On the TV in the corner they were playing the local Fox affiliate 11 o'clock news and it was so loud in the way TVs are loud in hospitals. I don't know if they do that for old people who tend to be overrepresented in these kind of settings or because every other step in the process of seeking out medical care is already so frustrating they figure what harm can one more sensory fuck you do.

The concept of the 11 o'clock news still existing felt anachronistic in and of itself which wasn't helping my feeling that I'd stepped out of time into this depressing and rundown hospital just a mile down the road from the even more depressing prison in the seventh richest town in Massachusetts. I don't think this hospital or the prison are meant for the actual residents of the rich town though. They probably go to a nicer hospital and nicer prison you and I don't have directions to.

Frannie was waiting with me and telling me about how she first heard the news about Roe at recess earlier that day. It was already going to have been an emotional day for her since it was her last day at this school and she recently accepted a different job in another town. I was proud of her but I also couldn't help but wonder if this would be a safer job for her to be in now as far as any hypothetical future school shootings. The Supreme Court had recently fucked with states' ability to regulate guns.

The Court had also just ruled that teachers have a right to pray publicly and lead students in prayer.

She said she and some of her colleagues stood there and cried together while the children they were responsible for ran around outside oblivious to the news and oblivious to everything. The last day of school is typically such a joyous day for everyone involved.

Well you're never going to forget this last day I said.

You have to try to joke in the emergency room to distract yourself from the weight of everyone around you involved in a dozen different kinds of tragedies.

She said that she definitely would not.

I asked if she and the other teachers thought to pray.

No we didn't pray she said.

Not out loud she said.

I asked her something like is it devastating for you how many awful people there are in the world or instead is it heartening how many good people there are in spite of that and she said she needed to think about that one for a while.

I wake up every day and think no one is going to stop this she said after some silence. No one? And then resign myself to that fact and start the whole process all over again.

I am not naive she said. I did not just learn about how the world works today. Over the past year. It's just that my stubborn belief in the goodness of people has been so hard to finally and utterly kill off. And it repairs itself like a slowly mending heart.

I don't know how many people are evil I said. Not most. But enough of them that the balance doesn't make a difference. They are worse than we are not.

The TV news was covering some of the protests going on around the country but only briefly then they switched to showing surveillance shots of suspects that the police needed our help finding for a series of property crimes around the Boston area. Some dumb shit standing there in a hat breaking a car window.

The day the news happened I had been leveled with fatigue but unable to nap and then after gorging myself doom scrolling I found myself short of breath when it was time to go to bed. Shortness of breath being one of the side effects of this new medication I've been taking that you're supposed to call your doctor about. I got actually scared that I might be dying for the first time in my life.

I know that I am dying of course but it's meant to be some time later on not right now. Never right now. That's not real.

I woke her up and sheepishly asked her to take me to the emergency room and so there we were. Something kept telling me not to bother in part because of the potential cost and in part because it's just kind of embarrassing to me to go to the emergency room unless you're bleeding out or have a broken limb or something.

A kind of fucked up masculinity at play there perhaps.

I kept apologizing for waking her up. On this day of all days. This is absurd I'm so sorry I said about a hundred times and I meant it about both things happening.

So the nurse came to get me with a wheelchair and I was like come on this is a bit much. I got in it anyway and she wheeled me literally ten yards like it was a gag. Like calling an Uber to get to your kitchen. She got me into the room and she asked me to take off my shirt and started applying all these sticky little things to me to do an EKG all the while asking me about my tattoos like the nurses who draw my blood always do and telling me about ones she wants to get herself.

Oh wow I said.

I know they're just trying to talk about something to make it all seem less awkward I'm not a dickhead.

Then she tells me she's only twenty for some reason and I thought to myself uh is that legal? To be that young. Not just in a hospital but anywhere.

She said she was still in training actually and I said oh that makes me feel a lot better and then she bent over to attach the wires to my heart and she had a big dangling golden cross necklace on so there was this fucking guy in my face yet again. Literally in my face. Also her cleavage. I'm ashamed to admit how I felt about that at a time like this but fortunately there was the guy I am supposed to repent to for such sins so that was convenient. The poison and the antidote.

I thought later about the two main things I got from my family which were this crippling indoctrination into Catholicism and a tendency to die young and how I never asked for either of them.

I declined the round trip in the wheelchair and walked myself back out to the waiting room and sat down and on the TV they were showing highlights of the annual greasy pole competition in Gloucester. Gloucester is a cute little seaside Massachusetts town which means it has a fishing industry and a debilitating opioid problem.

There was a long wooden pole jutting out off of a dock over the water that was doused in grease and a bunch of jabronis trying to make it to the end and grab a flag before spilling into the drink below. Most of them fell on their ass instantly.

The St. Peter's Fiesta is an event that's been going on since about the turn of the last century I read later. It was brought over from Sicily by the fishermen who immigrated to the area. It was meant as a celebration of their patron saint who protected them against storms at sea over the course of the year.

St. Peter is supposed to be the door guy in Heaven. The one checking the list of everything bad we've ever done. Normally I'd tease more out of that but I don't want to be thinking about any Catholic shit at this time. I've had quite enough of Catholic shit for the moment.

They should have never let us attain power. They had that one correct.

After about an hour waiting there in the shitty chairs listening to people cough and moan and whimper and watching the news explain how we should all be scared every second of our lives no one had come out to get me so I went to ask the gal at the desk if it would be much longer. She said oh yeah it's gonna be a real long wait. They're really busy back there she said. You're fucked basically she said.

I thought couldn't you at least lie to me a little bit here?

I figured if the machine saw that there was something seriously wrong with my heart they would have come out and told me by now because I'm still naive enough to believe things like that. I said let's get the fuck out of here and we did. We got the fuck out of there and went home and everything was basically fine and I went on to live for however much longer I am going to live.

On the walk out I saw an older woman sitting in a wheelchair in front of the TV with her head in her hands crying but I wasn't sure if it was emotional pain from the day's big news or whatever more routine physical pain she was dealing with. Probably both.

It has always struck me as a callous and careless feat of biological engineering that we can experience the two at once. And all manner of different kinds within either category.

You would have hoped that there would have been failsafes designed for when the emotional and physical signals overload like a circuit breaker but nonetheless here we are inside of these bodies and brains that we've borrowed for a little while. Our thousands of exposed nerves constantly attuned to everything and everyone trying to harm us. And so many of them out there. Who do we pray to to give thanks for that?

Something that was once potentially good

It never feels good sending off money to the federal government around this time of year but it has never felt as bad as it does today. I know I have paid to produce so much suffering throughout my entire life but there was always a plausible deniability baked in. Like how they put blanks in one of the firing squad rifles. Could be my money is going to school books or cancer research you could sort of lie to yourself before. But now there are no books being purchased and no research is being done.

I wonder how long it will take for the fruits of my specific labor to be processed into a neighbor's anguish? Watch as this brutal machinery transforms the written word into abductions. Something like bureaucratic sublimation. I don't know if they know how to track that sort of thing and if they ever did they must have fired everyone at that particular agency by now anyway.

I wanted to look up some details about firing squads just now and one of the first things that came up was an article in People magazine from a couple days ago.

"S.C. Man, Who Was Convicted of Killing a Cop, Chose This Upscale Final Meal Before His Firing Squad Execution" is the headline.

Upscale final meal is a new phrase for me to have to know and think about now.

"On the evening of Wednesday, April 9, he ate his last meal: a fine dining offer made up of a rib eye steak, mushroom risotto, broccoli and collard greens, with cheesecake for dessert and a sweet tea drink…"

"According to the AP, Mikal Mahdi cried out as the first bullets hit him, before flexing his arms and groaning."

Thank you for letting us know People magazine.

I have always despised these kinds of stories but apparently they remain very popular. I guess the publications think it's a good excuse to get readers riled up about what their tax dollars are being wasted on but it's usually the condemned man's steak not the state sanctioned killing.

I obviously revile capital punishment but I just had this strange new thought that I may not have ever had before which is that at least this man was given a trial before being disposed of by the government.

Remember the good old days when that was a given?

Mostly a given I mean.

"At around noon on April 14 2025, America ceased to have a law-abiding government," the Financial Times announced today.

"Some would argue that had already happened on January 20, when Donald Trump was inaugurated. On Monday, however, Trump chose to ignore a 9-0 Supreme Court ruling to repatriate an illegally deported man. He even claimed the judges ruled in his favour. The US president's middle finger to the court was echoed by his attorney-general, secretary of state, vice-president and El Salvador's vigilante president Nayib Bukele. The latter is playing host to what resembles an embryonic US gulag."

Embryonic US gulag is another of those new to me phrases.

"I said homegrowns are next," Trump told Bukele.

"The homegrowns. You gotta build about five more places."

Homegrowns.

How does that word make you feel? It makes my fucking skin crawl man. It makes me feel how it feels when you find maggots in the kitchen.

When you figure out what that smell behind the wall is.

They finally managed to come up with a slur for citizens that matches *illegals* in its grotesqueness.

I just saw a GoFundMe being shared around for Kilmar Abrego Garcia the innocent man being tortured in El Salvador by Trump and Bukele and all of their goons. Sorry I pointed out that he is innocent. I do not care that he is innocent. I do but you get it. No one either charged or convicted of a crime in the United States should be shipped off to be tortured in a foreign country.

I had two thoughts about that fundraiser which are that like every GoFundMe ever this one should not exist. It is being made to exist by our government.

The second thing is that I had this brief shudder over whether or not they would consider anyone donating to it as engaging in *material support of terrorism*. Would you put something like that past them at this point?

After that I read an interview with Deborah Lipstadt who was until recently Joe Biden's Special Envoy for Monitoring and Combating Anti-Semitism.

"To depict some of these people as martyrs and heroes is ludicrous," she said of students like Rumeysa Ozturk and Mahmoud Khalil who have been kidnapped by the government for the crime of opposing Israel's genocide.

They are no angels in other words.

"I'm not opposed to the administration rescinding the student visas of some of the people that they're rescinding the student visas of," she said. "But I just think it should be done properly, according to the laws of the country."

She just wants the disappearing and renditioning to be done in an orderly fashion. Still sounds pretty bad to me but I'm not an internationally renowned holocaust scholar like she is to be fair.

I have had this strange tension inside of me for a while now that I can't relieve myself of by turning it into words which is the course of care that I typically prescribe myself. When it is too early yet to have a drink that is. Something about how it feels to have been shouting for so long that we are already well on our way to fascism and in fact in many ways have always already been there and now that it has officially arrived a sense of my own obsolescence comes with it.

Suddenly everything I ever wrote feels as useless as a weather report from five years ago.

Or a shitty old flyer for a concert that has already happened.

Here's a post I just read:

"The reporter from MyPillow asked the White House press secretary why the president looks so healthy and robust…"

RIP David Foster Wallace you would have hated still being alive.

The president's doctor reported this week that Trump was 6'3 and 224 pounds. The measurements of a guard in the NBA. Marcus Smart's build in other words.

I suppose it makes sense that a lot of people would call the time of death on April 14. It is Ruination Day after all. The day "the iceberg broke and the Okies fled and the Great Emancipator took a bullet to the back of his head" as the song goes.

Perhaps at the very least we'll get an updated verse from Gillian Welch. If not maybe we can ask "A.I." to make one for us.

There was an article in the Times yesterday about how many students and teachers alike are using "A.I." to both complete and grade assignments

"Writing is one of the most challenging tasks for students, which is why it is so tempting for some to ask A.I. to do it for them. In turn, A.I. can be useful for teachers who would like to assign more writing, but are limited in their time to grade it."

I can't come up with the correct metaphor for how that makes me feel. I already used the thing about maggots earlier.

For some reason I keep thinking about an inert sex doll using a dildo. No not in a horny way.

Technically a kind of sex is happening there right? But it sort of removes the main point of the enterprise.

Ok here's a better metaphor I saw posted:

"I'm sorry but if your students use A.I. to write papers and you use A.I. to grade them zero school is happening. You are running together on a hamster wheel."

Zero school is happening.

And another:

"Even accepting the premise that A.I. produces useful writing (which no one should), using A.I. in education is like using a forklift at the gym. The weights do not actually need to be moved from place to place. That is not the work. The work is what happens within you."

I like that second one a lot but if you've spent enough time in the gym you know that the weights do actually yearn to be lifted. If you listen closely they are begging you to do it.

My elbows are fucked and I haven't been able to lift for a couple months so could be that's just a me thing.

Hold on I'll be right back.

I went outside and I saw my neighbor fucking around with the foundation of his home and I said hey buddy what have you got cooking over there and he said he was spackling it or whatever it is with some kind of repair goo for the cement. So it doesn't collapse. Kind of punting on that problem til later on.

I'm not sure if any of this "A.I." business is connected to anything else I'm talking about here. Aside from the fact that they're using it to decide who to kidnap and rendition or fire.

How about something along the lines of:

Democracy much like writing or making art is a discipline that must be practiced continuously rather than an achievement one unlocks?

Talk to any great guitar player and they will tell you they still do not know a thing about playing the guitar.

Meanwhile people on my Facebook can't get enough of those dog shit "A.I." action figure memes. They love this shit so much. They're having the time of their fucking lives posting them. What if I looked like this lol? What if I had three little toys that came with me?

Then instantly forgetting about it and dumping it on our doorsteps for us to have to reckon with. Like emptying the bucket of piss out the window onto the street below.

I'll be back in a few sorry hold tight. I gotta go out for a bit.

Ok I just got home from physical therapy. I sat there the whole time doing slow and exacting work trying to heal my malfunctioning body. Something that I'm worried I've already ruined beyond repair. But I'm just not gonna do all this shit man. I can't do this shit. Doing wrist curls with 2 lb. weights and shit. I'm sorry to everyone but mostly to me. Fuck it.

On the drive back I had to stop for a couple of school buses to let all the kids get off to cross the street to get home. Bopping around with their backpacks on. Not long after a bunch of ambulances and fire trucks came flying down the road and me and everyone else around all pulled over to let them pass. I kind of cried a little. I felt briefly like I was a part of something that was once potentially good.

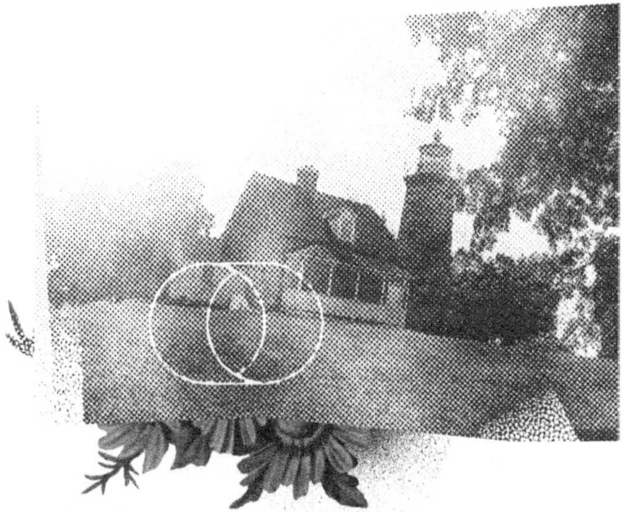

Now and at the hour of our death

The guy had really front-loaded the tour with the grisly showstoppers so about an hour in the bowl was mostly cashed in terms of murderous celebrity mansions and the sights of historic atrocities. Now the three of them sat in the back of the horse thing freelancing their own distraction.

The air smelling alternately of blooming star jasmine and humid sewage and horse shit. Literally and figuratively.

This is gross I know but do you kind of like the smell E__ said. Smearing sunscreen on her face.

Doing it kind of vomitously F__ thought.

The hay in it I mean. It reminds me of... Of being a child.

Or right now F__ said.

The horse was currently shitting and two children from the other tourist group riding along in the cart were delighted by this development. Pointing at the turds as they receded into the distance behind them. Being flushed down the pipe of the street with everything else on it.

Wait you grew up on a farm right A__ said.

Well sort of E__ said. It had been a working farm. My great-grandfather was... Well I don't know. Some kind of big guy. At some point. Back then. It was in the process of not being a farm anymore by the time I was old enough to know what anything was though. Being disassembled into just a house.

Farm entropy F__ said.

Sure. Farm entropy. There was a big little pig alive there still when I was in school and a sad old horse. And a corn field that was ten miles wide.

What was the horse called A__ said.

He was called Mr. Knees.

Mr. Knees.

I don't care for that A__ said.

I didn't know any better! I was a child.

It wasn't ten miles wide F__ said.

What? The farm? I don't know. Don't fact check my memories bitch she said.

I'm just saying. That would be an enormous farm. Especially one with one single horse.

What are you a land surveyor? Ok it wasn't that big. Fine. There were other horses before too but they all died from the... Or were sold. I don't know. It's just how everything seemed bigger when you were young. When you couldn't even reach the kitchen faucet. Or the doorknob.

When you couldn't get out of anywhere.

They were making their way down a block that was lined with massive nuttall oaks that seemed to grow parallel to the ground more than they grew upward. The guy had told them that was what the trees were called.

A squid digging headfirst into the floor of the deep ocean A__ thought. Scurrying to hide. Or to hunt. Both maybe. The agitated cloudy sand.

How old are the trees she asked the guy and he said they were older than anything. Well anything around here that has a name.

She looked over at F__ who was already going like alright buddy behind the guy's back. Give it a rest Mr. Spooky.

They had this idea to take seeds up to the moon in 1971. Apollo 14 the guy said. F__ was noticing a bulge at his hip as he turned back to talk at them that made him nervous. In fairness that wasn't uncommon around here. It was the most normal thing in the world.

So they took the seeds up to the moon and brought them back down again and planted them all over the country to... Well I don't know why actually. See if they would grow funny he said. Or not. Maybe just to have done it. There were two decent sized ones not far from here. Loblolly pines I believe. But the flood took them over he said. Washed them away. They left the plaques up for a while after but eventually the city came and took those down too.

E__ was intrigued by the idea of giving seeds a tour of space. Wondering what they thought all of that effort could possibly have imprinted on their lives as mature trees later on. Maybe it was bad for them. Like smoking cigarettes when you're newly pregnant. Which she newly was. And was doing. Not ready to quit yet because then everyone would know.

Furtive short puffs though that didn't technically count.

Nothing too strange happened to the rest of the trees by and large as far as I know but some of them started growing horizontally themselves the guy said. Maybe like they knew something other normal trees didn't. To stay close to the ground.

Shit my phone is dying A__ said.

All of their phones were dying.

Everyone's phones everywhere were dying.

Specifically in this instance however the phones were dying on account of them having posted so many stories along the tour.

Of ornate tombs for example.

***

He was on an outing with friends all picnicking on the grass of a red lake telling him it was too cold to swim this early in the season and he laughed and said he was going to be fine and then plunged so elegantly and swam down and down and from there the muck and the weeds knew he had arrived and knew of him and grasped for him at the bottom of his plummet. Gathered him in close. As if he'd announced his visit ahead of time.

A voice was talking now to him saying to give in. A friendly voice mind you. These types of voices are always welcoming at first. Like the guys lying in wait for marks in the shadow of the old Cathedral.

It's basically fine the voice said. It's nothing. It's like anywhere else over here. It's walking through a door. Or a window. Like going out a window is what it is like.

How many stories high?

I don't know we don't have stories down here man the voice said.

Sorry sorry I got annoyed for a second it said. It's just… We don't measure it like that. It's more like when you have to cross through into another state to get to a store that's actually in your state. How the lines are drawn weird like that sometimes. A jigsaw puzzle. No one remembers why. Do you know what I'm trying to say? How the roads up there were designed by horses. How Boston is for example.

I've never been to Boston he said.

You know what I mean it said.

Do you promise me I'll be ok he said and the voice said you will be essentially fine. Just swim a little deeper for a minute real quick and let go.

Later when he was being interviewed by the newspaper he said that when he heard the words let go he pretty much left his body and went into this… Other dimension.

It was like ejecting from a fighter plane upside down he said. The parachute erupting beneath you and then collecting you up as you fell.

Thrust into a place where he was an infinitesimal part of this self-sustaining light source.

No not the sun.

It wasn't a lighthouse either so don't think about a lighthouse.

It was the most incredible amazing feeling he said. And then. And then. And then. It was all one consciousness.

He told the reporter he knew everything.

***

When you die and you are going to be placed into the family tomb or whatever tomb it happens to be there's a waiting period the guy said. Jostling the horse's reins. After one person has been locked into the tomb the next person has to wait one year and one day to get lodging inside even if they die in the meantime.

Where do they go to wait A__ said.

Let's say dear nana dies and you brick her up inside and etch her name onto the wall. You can't disturb her transitioning for that entire time the guy said. If old dad's poor heart breaks once she's gone and he decides he wants to follow shortly behind her he's going to have to hold on for his turn.

He's going to have to be patient for the iron door to squeak again.

Where does he go meanwhile E__ asked.

She had this feeling like she wanted to hug the horse so badly. Throw her arms around its neck and never let go.

Around the perimeter of the garden there are coffin-sized drawers to wait in the guy said. See? Right there.

Like a death waiting room E__ said.

Just like that he said.

They even have TVs in there playing the Fox News F__ said and A__ said wait really?

Don't worry though the guy said. It's so humid and it gets up to 300 degrees inside the tombs. So your grandparents are a pile of bones before long.

Oh thank god F__ said. So it's like a slow cooker? The meat falls off the bone.

More or less the guy said.

There has to be an order to things. There has to be law. Even for the dead.

***

Did he remember what he saw?

What?

The guy who drowned. Did he remember?

He said he remembered his entire life if that's what you mean. He saw his entire life. And he said when he saw his life he also... Well when he was looking at it the only thing that was different is that he knew how he was but he also knew how everybody else was. Feeling. In every moment of his life. And their lives. And they knew his life too. They saw him. And it was like. The most comforting thing.

Everything?

So he said.

Even all the times he was jacking off?

He didn't talk about jacking off. But then...

Because I worry about that sometimes.

Part of the light...

What if they can see us? My poor grandmother.

He didn't say anything in the interview about jacking off stop it. But he said it was the most euphoric incredible feeling he's ever felt.

So like jacking off.

Shut up! He said he felt peace. Calm. Happiness. Wonder. Knowing everything. Being part of everything. He said you know everything down there.

And then the voice said to him you have to go back. The guy said I don't want to. This is way better than being part of the dryness he said. On the land of Earth he said which was a weird way to say it he knew.

And it said no you have to go back. Thank you for your contributions and all but we're going in a different direction. Like that. Professional but firm. HR had gotten involved. And then he got heaved back up like the weeds bench-pressed him into the sky and he landed back on the shore and he said getting vacuumed back into his body was the worst feeling he has ever felt. Worse than a compound fracture which he had also had when he was younger he said.

But he woke up?

Well yes how else would we know about what happened?

I would think it would be the opposite. That it would be euphoria to return to your body. Like being born but you're aware of it. No crying this time. No screaming. No blood.

Right? He said he thought the pain was because he had experienced this period of being out of his body and being and seeing everything...

Maybe it's like coming down.

And then he woke up and they were giving him mouth to mouth on the shore.

Who was?

Some girl. Some girl in her little shorts. He said he will never forget how her lips tasted on his.

What did they taste like?

He didn't say. Honey maybe. So then the girl and his friends asked him what had happened down there and later he told the interviewer guy that in the immediate aftermath he had lied to them. The thing is there was no question he was going to lie as soon as he came back he said. No negotiation. He knew he was going to be a liar now. That was who he was and was going to be.

He said he lied because he didn't want to tell anyone what the world really is. Because he was embarrassed to have this knowledge. Like a child who learns too early about what his parents are up to in the dark. Or why one of them is never there anymore. Where grandpa went off to.

But also because he knew they wouldn't believe him.

He lived with this knowledge his whole life and then... Well. Not his whole life. But he'd never heard anyone talk about anything like this and he didn't want to tell anyone because he thought that he was being crazy. And then he read a book about someone who had experienced the same thing. It described exactly what happened to him he said.

He could've just actually been making it all up though right?

But the way he described it was completely beautiful. So even if that's not what really happened I can just believe that. I can believe that.

Something about the chemicals in your brain maybe though? When you're about to die. Somebody said that makes you feel good. That the body has certain...

Yeah. Sure. But then I was so tired and so...

Who was tired?

Me in real life. When I was watching this video I'm telling you about.

Oh I didn't realize it was a video. That makes it... uh. That sort has a deflating effect. On my suspension of disbelief.

No. Stop. And there was music playing in the background. It was very calming. Like massage music. But scary kind of. A haunted massage parlor. It was like I was in a trance. Then I put down my phone. So I said I'm just going to try to be at peace and at one with myself. And I'm going to just think about moments from my life the way he described it. So I fell asleep and I had dreams where I was choosing to watch moments in my life. I became like him.

What if it was like streaming and you couldn't ever decide on a part of your life to watch? Too much to choose from. Abundance wise. Or all they had available were seasons of your life you know sucked ass. The production had run out of money and you were just sort of in stasis. Zero character development.

No it wasn't like that. It was very comforting. To learn about. Not learn... But to hear about. At that time in the morning when I had insomnia. It's a nice thought.

Well aside from the part where they watch us jack off.

It's not like watching you.... Well yeah. I mean if you go up into the light you're probably going to have to watch yourself jerking off. Fine.

Haha. I don't want to watch myself.

Who then? Who do you want to watch doing that?

***

Mr. Knees was so tall E__ said to no one. Changing the subject.

That was why he was called that. You would stand next to him and just come up to his knees. My grandfather was trying to sell him before he got sick not long after that. The horse got sick I mean. My grandfather too. Everybody got sick right around then. I remember we went in to say goodbye to him. I think I even prayed for him. I prayed for a horse. I cried more when the horse died than my grandfather. It's all coming back now.

Do horses have souls she said.

I don't know she thought. Everyone thought. Each of them retreating to their own corners. Not wanting to think about that.

A__ was snapping another picture of a particularly large grasping oak. Trying to imprison its elderly fluidity in stopped time.

Fuck fuck fuck she said as her phone finally died while taking one of its final shots.

Now what?

They were clomping alongside a set of tracks that lined the middle of the avenue but no street car or regular car had passed by them in the last hour or more which felt incorrect.

This is why we couldn't find a trolley to take us over here E__ said.

When we were young we'd have our birthday parties on some of the trolley lines the guy said. Have cake inside and everything.

This made the two children perk up for the first time since the turds.

Did you ever come up this way E__ asked and the guy looked back at her like she was a stupid asshole. Like she had just asked him whether he drank water out of the toilet.

A__ was instinctively looking at her dead phone now. Forgetting there was no point to it anymore. Staring at the black screen out of habit. Hoping that it hadn't actually died and there was some spark of life left in it. She caught a glimpse of her reflection in the blackness and thought she looked so old.

The sound of a trolley horn and finally here came one from around the bend up ahead. They figured they could take it to head back to where they were living but they'd have to jump out of the carriage right now to catch it. They'd have to make a run for it. They'd have to let go.

But not break

It was humid in the bedroom when she woke me up around 1:30 to say that it was over. I had determined earlier in the night that it wasn't going to do anyone any good for me to watch the results come in slowly at first then all of a sudden and so I took a little something to help me sleep that my adrenaline was now in heated competition with. I rolled over and opened the laptop and said the only thing I can ever really think of to say about anything that ever happens anymore which is *goddamnit*.

Then I lied and told her everything was going to be alright.

I slept a few more hours the rest of the night but none of them consecutively. Topped myself off with another pill and regretted that later on swimming in a daze through the record breaking 85 degree November weather. It felt fitting to be uncomfortable in another unnatural way.

This too?

This too.

When I saw the look in her eyes in the morning I felt a wave of guilt wash over me that I still haven't shaken. As if I were personally responsible for all of this. I suppose I am in the way we all are. Having failed to stop this. We couldn't even maintain the already shitty status quo.

Not even that?

Not even that.

I raked the leaves for an hour to have some kind of purpose and when I was done and admiring my handiwork the wind came in slowly at first then all of a sudden and sent me back to square one.

I was surprised at how surprised I was. How surprised I still am.

A kind of embarrassment. Personally and nationally speaking.

I feel so naive a friend told me.

On top of all that the Democrat fundraising texts didn't even stop coming.

My first indication that something was off was when a cop at my polling place made a friendly joke to me about my Every Time I Die t-shirt and I responded in a jovial manner. I should not have done that. I am sorry for throwing the vibes off.

I feel an empty loss for words right now similar to when there's a shooting big enough we all have to talk about it. No one learning anything. No point trying anymore. Just a blanket of sadness.

I'm not supposed to say that kind of thing though. I'm supposed to talk about finding community and solidarity locally and building from there and yes I believe that is vital but I do not right now today believe that it is important enough to matter in anything but the long bending arc of the moral universe as the saying goes.

How much further can this thing bend?

Terroir

They had been bombed so frequently by now that even the children had come to know the category of missile by the sound they made as they fell or the size of the hole they left behind. The sensibility of a sommelier.

We had it coming

> *We had it coming*
> —Luke O'Neil

We had it coming.
    Excerpted from *We Had It Coming* by Luke O'Neil (2025)

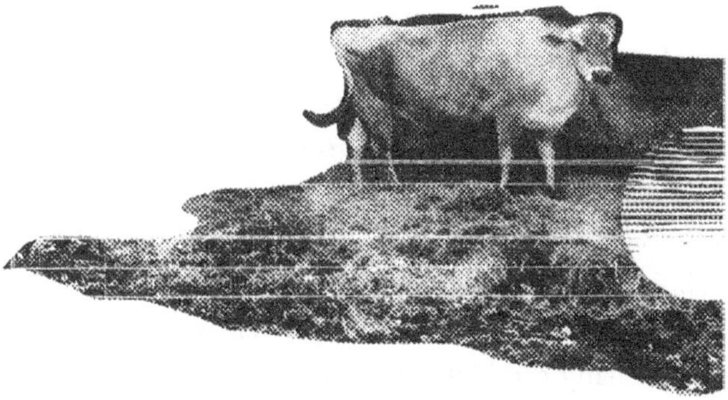

Updates from my backyard March 2025

Technically speaking it wasn't quite spring just yet but this little rabbit didn't know that. It was running undisciplined routes across the yard like a rookie slot receiver and now came back around for another sniff of the dead garden near where I sat thinking about the concept of spring. In this iteration it had its mouth stuffed with big sprigs of desiccated straw that jutted out either side and made it look like it was wearing a fake mustache. Like it was doing a bit. She was doing a bit. Gathering building material for a nest I presumed. I moved as slowly as I could to get close enough to take a picture thinking I would send it to my girlfriend. We had had a fight last night and I hoped it would remind her how gentle I mostly am. The fucking rabbit wouldn't pose correctly though and I was trying not to make any sudden moves that would scare her off. Scaring a rabbit off is so easy to do. One of the easiest things in the world. I took three or four snaps before my looming spooked her and texted them out and waited a few impatient minutes for a bunny and kissy face emoji in response and now felt square as regards that. That someone believed that I was still a good man. I looked over toward the neighbor's yard and felt the absence of two tall thin arborvitae they had had cut down recently and got pissed off about it anew. I wanted to give the guy a piece of my mind. I always imagined they looked like they belonged somewhere else. California perhaps. Art Deco trees. Out of time. But after they were gone I realized they belonged right where they were here in New England. I looked them up later to get the name right and this is so stupid but arborvitae obviously means the tree of life. I probably should have been able to work that one out on my own via 8th grade Latin. God it must have been so much easier to name things then. Back whenever they named everything. Walking around pointing at plants and animals and rivers that no one had ever bothered to call what they are properly called before. To differentiate one from the other. I thought I should name my bunny in question here. That I could name every single one that had ever run away from me if I had to.

The end of all wanting

It smelled like someone might have left the gas stove on so I muted the news and got up off of the couch and went into the kitchen to poke my snout around.

Everything seemed to be switched off as best as I could tell.

The bulldozers were busy pummeling along the border they were saying a minute ago. In a place a lot of people didn't want them to be bulldozing. A place of some import. A consecrated place. I was only half paying attention but it seemed bad. A matter of something despoiled.

When I was done checking I got worried I had turned the stove back on somehow so I had to do the same routine over again in the exact same order. One more time again but no more after that. Controlled enough to not do it the third time.

Half of a thing of macaroni and cheese from yesterday there wilting in the pot and becoming more and more yellow. An exceptional yellowness. So yellow it wasn't yellow anymore.

Who closed last night?

The odor of rotten eggs and sulfur was all of a sudden overwhelming. The only thing I ever really heard about sulfur is that it is supposed to be what Hell smells like but then again how could anyone know that? Who reported on that?

Dante I guess.

I opened the fridge and there were near to rotting eggs and near to expiring milk in there so that complicated things in terms of my investigation olfactory wise.

I didn't have it in me to check the pest traps under the sink. I knew that there were cockroaches thriving and multiplying down there in the damp dark but as long as I didn't see them it wasn't my concern at the moment.

I had spent so many months fighting against them that I had given up. Spraying them and poisoning them and crushing them with my feet in their oily hundreds and furious as they insisted upon struggling to survive so relentlessly.

And for what? Just to live? To reproduce?

It made me feel like they knew something I didn't.

What kind of life can that be?

I'd have given anything to wipe them all from the face of the earth. Or at least the specific earth I was on top of.

After that the only other thing I could think of to do next was to pick up my phone and type what dose agas leek smel li.e and it told me that because natural gas is odorless the guys down at the gas company had to add the artificial smell to it because otherwise we wouldn't know it was killing us when it was killing us. It was considered more professional to provide a warning. An alarm sort of.

I never thought of my nose as an alarm before but that is exactly what a nose is.

An antenna wriggling this way and that.

My next thing I did was to post I thikn the.re's a gas leak in my hosue and pretty quickly I got hit with a dozen variations of we know lol and yeah we've read your posts from my dickhead friends and the people who live in the computer and molest me.

Go outside right now one of them said after a minute or two of me standing there reading about how much I sucked and I said alright and immediately forgot and kept scrolling on my phone in the light of the gaping fridge door beeping now in another kind of alarm.

I saw that they had lowered the flag to half-mast at Fenway Park because a beloved knuckleballer had died and they had lowered the flag to half-mast at Guantanamo Bay because a senator who loved torturing people had died and I saw that Lolita the orca had died following a medical procedure at the aquarium and I felt sad about that even though I had never heard of this particular orca. It didn't say if they lowered the theme park flag for Lolita. If the mascots had to stand around solemnly in the big fish hats they make them wear.

It's always sad when something big dies I thought.

Killer whales were actually dolphins I read recently. More or less. Within that whole area. That spectrum of life. They were also supposed to be waging a war on yachts all around the world. Everyone was making it a whole thing. Injecting their own politics into the instincts of the dying sea. I think more likely the orcas were just kind of thrashing around and lashing out at whoever they could reach and being so powerful that can be a problem for anything floating nearby.

The rest of us on land are safe everyones seems to have decided. What can they do to us here?

Ryan came out of his room waving his hand in front of his face and said what is that smell do you smell that and I said that I did. What is it he said and I said it's maybe a gas leak situation.

The gas company puts that artificial smell in there so we'll smell it right away I told him. We gotta go outside right now I said. Adopting a mantle of authority. Pulling a bouquet of capability out of my ass like a magician.

Don't call me an idiot Ryan said and I said I didn't call you an idiot did I?

I did think it though so I said I was sorry just in case I was misremembering the previous ten to twenty seconds.

That wasn't right of me to think Ryan I said.

Say he said.

Say I said.

I accept your apology he said.

Idiot I thought.

Come on man he said.

Now we were outside on the porch and he was trying to light a joint he had produced by sleight of hand. The lighter nearly cashed it seemed like.

Flick flick flick the lighter said as the neighborhood coyote cried in the near distance.

Was that him he said and I said yeah I think so.

The same one?

How many coyotes can there be in this part of the world?

I don't know he said. Ten thousand?

That sounds about right I said having no idea either way.

There hadn't been as much reporting on the local coyotes compared to the orcas because they were mostly only attacking people and not boats.

Flick flick flick.

Will you light that thing already I said.

Flicking it again and then again and then once more before it took purchase and the flame lit up his face.

He took a drag off of the spliff and its cherry combusted oddly and I thought of a wet log on a campfire and said maybe let's go out into the street a bit more buddy. Waving my arm underhand like an usher and we walked up a ways and stood there under the punishing street light that floods my bedroom like a Broadway stage and were quiet for a minute or two within the smoking.

Do you hear that he said.

What are they chanting?

Some helicopters were wafting just there over the park. So many I started to sort of worry about them crashing into each other.

A vortex compelling them inward. Crashing like that if you can imagine it.

That must be where the protests are Ryan said. I was gonna go he said and I said me too. I had meant to go to that I said. It's funny they were just saying something about it on the news beforehand I said. About how bad it all was. But necessary also. Bad but necessary. Unfortunate was the word they said.

It started to rain kind of weird. Kind of sideways. We stood there not seeking cover for a minute or two. Dumber than dogs.

Do you remember our first night here he said. Neither of us had a bed frame and we slept on the floor on our raggedy mattresses.

My biggest worry was a ghost was going to come kill us that night he said.

We hadn't been hanging out much lately so I think he was taking this as a bonding moment and I accepted it. I gave into it.

Why did you think there would be a ghost?

Look at the place. Slouching like it is. I wasn't sure if the house might be haunted. It was our first night.

I had forgotten about that I said. Most houses are not haunted though you know that right?

Doesn't mean ours isn't he said. 99.9% of all houses in the world are probably not haunted but if yours is well now they've got you by the balls.

It was all fine though that night he said. There ended up being zero ghosts that night.

Just the roaches.

The god damned roaches he said.

What is that banging sound he said.

Inside? It sounds like the washing machine. Did you leave it on?

He said that he had.

That's maybe not good in terms of the whole alleged gas deal we have going on here I said. Thinking what a time for this guy to finally do his laundry. I had once caught him flushing fistfuls of beach sand down the toilet. Just to see how good it swallowed he said.

We walked a little further upstage and Roger emerged in his yard lit up by the street light and still digging his row of graves. Sweating his ass off in the wet autumn chill by the look of it.

What is that about Ryan said elbowing me doing the conspiratorial whisper thing and also in the conspiratorial whisper thing I said that I had asked him what it was about yesterday and he assured me it was merely symbolic.

Symbolic of what?

Handing me the joint now.

Well I didn't let him get fully into it all. I wasn't in the right headspace for that sort of thing. So to speak. His brand of horse shit.

Hello boys Roger yelled over and we waved. I hid the weed behind my back out of reflex for no reason.

How goes the gravedigging Ryan said.

It's a tough business he said.

Good luck with the holes Ryan said and Roger said God bless you fellas and then something quieter I couldn't hear.

He kept stabbing the hell out of the earth and we walked up a ways to wait under the umbrella branches of the big red oak. Glancing around for the coyote. Listening mostly.

It was five in the morning and I woke up to hear this banging banging banging Ryan said.

What?

Like someone knocking at the door.

Like in The Raven?

No not like that really. Nothing to do with that. But I didn't know what it was. I went downstairs and nobody was at the door and I still heard the banging. So I went outside and looked around and I saw this woodpecker.

How did you see it in the dark?

It wasn't dark. It was the morning. The dawn. I didn't know it was a woodpecker at the time I just saw some bird. On the side of the house. Then it flew up and out. But I noticed what it looked like.

What did it look like?

Like a woodpecker.

Like in the cartoon?

No you idiot Ryan thought but I didn't call him on it.

It was white and black. Medium sized.

Medium compared to what?

The average bird.

Are bluebirds supposed to be exciting to see or not I said because I see them all the time in the yard these days. They're very striking I said but I don't know if they're just basically some guy as far as bird people think. People who know what birds are what.

Yeah I think that's right. Some random guy. Of birds.

Did you chase it off?

Yeah. I said hey! Hey bitch!

What did it say?

It said stop the bulldozing. What do you think it said?

You know what I mean.

It said nothing. Tweeted nothing. It flew off briefly and then circled back. I saw it in the tree that reaches toward the house later. It hopped along the branch onto the roof.

That tree wants to smash clear through into the house so badly he said. You can kind of feel it. Wanting that.

Trees do not want things I said.

99.9% of all trees probably do not want things he said.

Do you ever kind of feel like you're on a stage? Or being watched I said.

No I don't think things like that.

Me neither I was just making sure you also didn't. What do they want? These birds.

I think a couple things. I think they do that to try to mate. But it's not mating season. Maybe they're looking for insects.

Incest?

Insects.

It's like when you see guys tailgating at a football game he said. When they jump off the van into the table face first to show girls and their dads how tough they are.

Is it like that you think?

To get laid. The only reason to do anything.

How is Roger over there digging graves going to get himself laid?

Maybe he's digging up his wife.

Buddy no.

I don't know. Maybe he's like paying homage to having gotten laid in the past? Doing it for someone from before. To honor them?

I would like to think there comes a time in your life when fucking doesn't matter anymore I said. It sounds sad but it has to feel like a kind of clemency when it ends right? Innocent at last of lust. Of baseness.

For you maybe Ryan said.

Now some sirens were screaming toward us or maybe just near us or maybe the entire other way away from us and I asked Ryan if he had called 911 and he said that he had not and I thought well this is convenient timing on their part so we walked back up onto the porch to wave them down to come and save us. To sort of drop a pin. Ryan lit a cigarette and was now double fisting and waving his arms around like a beacon like a guy who works on the tarmac and we waited and watched the helicopters hovering closer and closer and closer.

But not forever

When it was newly twilight and we had been sitting together alone and no lights in the house had yet been turned on I would often say with the full voice the whole place is dark! and she would chuckle every time. Every single time. Not even humoring me. I think that's what he was always carrying on about. Not just in that song but in all of his songs. Not just in his songs but in all of the songs ever written. The things that later will be worth our mourning.

A desecration

The kids and my sisters had convinced me to upload her into the infernal contraption. They had all pitched in and got me one as a gift. As a transitional sort of deal.

My nephew handled the computer part of it. We were all proud of him for how much computer he was doing at school so I felt it was only right to let him chip in in his own way.

So there it sat on the mantle next to the ashes and some of the sturdier leftover flowers they took back from the funeral home for me.

She was never perfect I probably don't need to tell you. You know how she was. We hadn't had a very good last couple of years there toward the end. But from time to time I thought about turning it on. Turning her on. Not like that my goodness. Whatever the terminology is. Just as a test. To see how it worked. If it felt real.

Just talk to it they said.

Just try to pretend they said.

Alright.

Alright fine.

I still spread out the quilt your mother gave us on the couch when I have dinner in front of the TV I told her. Even now. I load the dishwasher the way you used to. God you would get so mad about that. Make the bed most days too.

The light inside of it was glowing. Like it was processing this new information.

It let out a shrill beeping. The sound of a fire alarm and then her voice.

Are you seriously smoking inside of the house right now?

Watertown, Massachusetts

I am sitting in a waiting room right now none of us ever want to be inside of crying about an old friend I'm not entirely sure is even gone yet. The telephone game both figurative and literal going on among friends. I sat and sat and remembered after some time that I could just call him to clarify the matter which I did. Hey man are you alive? Just checking. No answer though. It said the mailbox of the person I was calling was currently full so I texted instead. I was hoping that this was all a misunderstanding but I felt the curious mix of shame and devastation that I had just texted a dead man. I guess I was expecting some kind of miracle.

I noticed the last time we texted he had sent Nollaig shona duit and I said Happy Christmas to you too old buddy.

And then two years of nothing.

He was from Ireland but had been here for twenty five years or more working in the hospitality business in Boston and he hired me for a restaurant job I would have for many years that changed my life in ways both good and bad. I had some of the best and worst times of my life with this man. Sitting in the closed down restaurant all night chain smoking under the oven vents. Driving across the city at 4 in the morning to get another bag that neither of us really wanted and certainly did not need.

That's not true. We wanted it very badly in the moment. More than anything. So that nothing would ever end. Not just borrowing happiness from tomorrow to spend today but borrowing happiness from the rest of our lives.

I cannot believe we lived through some of that shit and now I guess one of us did not?

He was off the sauce for many years after we no longer worked together and I was very proud of him for that. While sober he was one of the more charming and hospitable people I knew. He was always sort of my boss in the way that someone who was once your boss and is a bit older is always your boss. He was proud of me too for my writing accomplishments despite not ever having any clue about how online media or social media worked. I had to show him how to use Instagram like he was eighty years old.

He lived around the corner and would have us over for the most lovely dinners. He knew so much about wine. He'd delight in pouring us important sounding bottles and not have any for himself during the good years there.

I'm not going to sugarcoat it he struggled very badly with substance abuse. Most of us did then or still do now. Oftentimes you probably wouldn't want to be around him unless you were that wasted and maybe not even then but that is how that all goes. A nice person can become an unbearable one so quickly. I have so many friends like that. Maybe that's me too. I don't think so but I wouldn't know would I? That's the other version of me and we are at odds with one another.

It all feels even stranger because just before I heard that my friend may or may not have passed I had been having a little cry about David Lynch and then my own David was either dead or was not.

Schrödinger's drinking buddy.

Restaurant families like the one we were a part of are a fractured fragile thing and I don't know if I know anyone who would know for certain right now. My one friend said their old co-worker said it happened this morning. I hope it's not true. It would be awkward if he has to read this and be like what the hell man? I hope he still can.

I wrote that yesterday and now I know he cannot.

I posted the news to Facebook and everyone said how much he made them care about the fine details of working in a restaurant. How he made them more of a professional. He did that for me too. Restaurant labor is terrible in many ways but hospitality is something different. That's a thing you can take pride in. That's humanity.

And now I'm sitting in another kind of room no one ever wants to be in.

It is such a disorienting feeling when someone you care about but hadn't talked to that much in a couple of years dies suddenly because there is now a freshly dug hole inside of you and yet the day to day routine of your life has not been altered one bit. A new kind of absence has taken over for an older different shaped absence and the two are in conflict. Trying to fit a triangle shaped sadness into a rectangle shaped sadness.

It's 0° right now in Massachusetts in the coldest month in recorded history.

A friend texted me a couple days later about his own recent experience with a friend who had died by suicide and I said one thing I can't figure out is whether or not I have cried sufficiently. I have wept multiple times but I stopped after three or so days I said. What is that?

Is that enough?

The nightmares about it haven't stopped though.

Another old friend called and I said the first day or two I just wanted to know what specifically had happened because we think information is an antidote to suffering and then we found out the details and I wished I hadn't ever heard that shit.

Sometimes it's best not to know.

I can't help but relate it to when my father died but I suppose that's not surprising from me the little bitch with an eternally dead and dying dad who I kept texting for a while after he wasn't there to respond ever again.

I'm doing that to my friend right now too I suppose by writing this.

Hey buddy I cried for three days after you went over. Not bad right? Pretty respectable. Was that more or less than you would have expected?

After your memorial a bunch of the old gang stood at the door of the Mount Auburn chapel and hugged and lied to one another about how good we all still looked.

It was a very lovely ceremony by the way. Everyone said that it was very lovely.

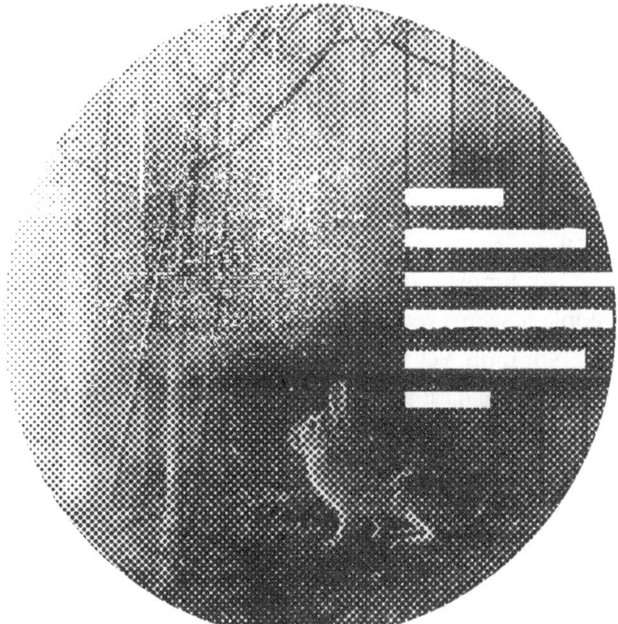

The long drop below

The bulk of the experts were in agreement that it was officially authoritarianism now. It technically counted as that. They had been batting the idea around for some time but by this late in the game had finally reached a consensus. The authors and academics and so forth. Many of them reporting as much from abroad having long since absconded.

It is imperative that you fight back they warned us.

Ok thanks man. Thank you for the advice.

Authoritarianism is fairly boring I have come to learn.

Not for everyone no. Not by any stretch. For some people it seems really bad.

Not quite yet for me though.

And wasn't it always so?

You mostly still get to walk around wherever you like. No one ever tells you about that part. Go to work. Get pissed off in traffic. You get to go to the store. Need to I should say. I gotta have my yogurts!

You can warmly greet your neighbors as per usual. Maybe not talk too in depth with them about anything of substance as a precaution as far as down the line is concerned but still.

Observing the comings and goings of the birds in your backyard remains free of charge. As does the feel of the sun warm on your face when it occasionally shines.

They can boil the earth slowly but they can't yet control the daily weather haha.

If they could they definitely would have announced it by now. They're far too stupid not to blurt out that they could do that. They must not even be close enough to feel comfortable lying about it right to our faces so that's a relief of a kind.

They have basketball on TV I should mention. The Celtics fucking blew it but there was in fact unrelated basketball on.

So loud in the stadiums.

DE-FENSE! etc.

This morning in particular in my corner of all of this it was the kind of cold and humid where the doors were closing weird. That hadn't changed either. How oppressive humidity is. The main door chittering like a bad knee going down the stairs. The hinges whinging about a job that they had been perfectly content to perform for quite some time.

Doors and joints do not have emotions or labor standards I know that.

I fumbled and flicked the light switch I don't normally hit and it briefly lit up someone else's kitchen. A moment later I fixed it and then it was just my same old shit.

My familiar kitchen under authoritarianism.

The coffee maker anticipating me in the dark of dawn.

Coffee was getting more expensive I suppose.

Coffee makers do not anticipate things I know that also.

I wandered away from it all and into the half bathroom and the bright bulbs above the mirror helped me convince myself I looked like a man ten years younger than I am for as long as I could hold my breath. I pulled my hoodie up over my head and played boxer. Flexed a little under the bulk of it.

I wondered for some reason how the actor Tom Hardy was faring. Wherever it is he is from. God he was so handsome. That was also still true under authoritarianism I imagined.

Everyone is becoming so coiled and sharp and ugly now so when you come across something persistently beautiful it's like a fleeting overdose.

Which you can't really do anymore without significant effort. Not with anything you'd want to overdose on.

You can dream as per usual. About anything you want. Someone who once loved you waiting at the bar for you to walk in the customary five minutes late and half turning toward the door when they sense you. Smiling like a searchlight.

A playful punch in the arm.

Splitting the mussels. Dipping the toasted bread into the leftover broth.

Might want to keep the dreams to yourself depending on the circumstances.

Reevaluate your relationship with your therapist too. They mostly want the cash upfront of late.

The flower shop down the road was open every other day and so I brought some home for my wife yesterday. Wives still appreciate flowers under authoritarianism.

I had just been to the dentist earlier in the week too so it wasn't like we didn't need to care for our teeth and bodies anymore. It wouldn't make sense for them to want everyone's teeth to fall out. How would that serve the cause?

Even the fake idea of the cause.

It did feel kind of weird being pretend tortured like that for a bit. You could let your mind wander regarding their tools in your mouth.

People nevertheless had to try to live and to make a living yes but just between you and I we were long already fucking dead.

Suspended in mid-air after running off the side of a cliff. Most of us not even looking back at the camera for the sake of the bit. Not self aware enough to know that there was a camera in the first place.

Or the long drop below.

Maybe those scholars and all of them knew. Writing books about what's to become of us from I don't know Ottawa or Helsinki. Somewhere cold and imaginary like that.

What will happen to me specifically though?

What at long last will become of me?

What will happen to *me*?

I keep catching myself having this feeling like well surely this cannot stand. Something will be done. A distinctly American hubris.

Tom Hardy is from the UK. I just thought of that. I suppose each of us has to suffer in our own way.

For you

On your timeline it's still the second quarter of a game your favorite team lost last night.

Activists are protesting the coming execution of a dead man the governor will soon decline to pardon.

On your timeline it's still Halloween and all the skeletons and princesses are giddy with childish gluttony.

There's a beautiful beach town unbothered by a looming storm. No cars stacked atop of one another like felled dominoes.

Nothing has happened anywhere.

On your timeline a friend is wearing last week's smile in a selfie she felt insecure about.

A movie no one went to see is about to premiere.

A party you weren't invited to is in full swing.

On your timeline an exhausted journalist in a bright blue vest is wandering amidst rubble that isn't smaller rubble under a sky clear of drones that haven't arrived.

A mother has yet to turn against God.

On your timeline I'm complaining about a delayed flight that has long since taken off and left me somewhere I'm not coming back from.

Do you remember how it felt when we still thought we had a chance?

Humans

He was in the garage jigsaw-puzzling the architecture of the bones. After some doing he looked upon his works and thought well that's sort of spooky. Not frightening yet but still. He rifled through the boxes and coolers of bullshit he had stashed out here from when he had last had to move in a hurry and went back to work fitting the joints and then stuffing it all with fistfuls of viscera and organs and when he had done that it still looked somehow slightly lacking. He couldn't quite put his finger on it. Like all the meat had gone bad instantaneously. All of it everywhere. Never mind though he evened out the spread of gaseous organs from tip to tail and it was just about as ugly as you please but nonetheless wanting. Goddamnit he said and then laughed at himself. He fixed a two way hose rig and hydrated the guts with a taste of his own hot pumping fluid which yet again didn't sufficiently alter the level of sin and not knowing what to do and almost ready to punt on the whole thing he wrapped and dressed the entire heaving wound of the mess in some discarded skin and peppered it with miscellaneous hair he had lying around from another project and then feeling himself now kind of in the rhythm of the zone of creation he painted it with all of the hues of the universe and then plopped in the glistening globs of the eyes and brightened them into pools of infinity and reddened the lips with the blush of a billion burning stars and curled them up just so over the skull's jagged hungry jaw and placed one of his own stabbing instruments in its grip to test out how it might be held later on when both officially existed and whispered something into its ear and he was after all of this labor satisfied. Finally it was the appropriate amount of terrifying.

First they came 2

First they came for the socialists which was pretty funny to be honest because they were mean to me online all the time. Then they randomly stopped there lol. Just before my ass. What are the odds of that? Welp back to normal.

A whole thing of pasta salad

A whole thing of pasta salad in the heaviest ceramic bowl you've ever seen on a weak fold out table. The tinfoil half-on and a wooden spoon poking out.

Penne lemon olive oil red wine vinegar cherry tomatoes green pepper red onion cucumber kalamata olives.

Feta souring in the sun.

Flies broadcasting the coordinates.

A greasy paper plate with the light blue trim resting leftover hell-blackened burgers and dogs no one else as of yet has been shameless enough to poke their noses into.

Lemony bug spray sweat on the back of your neck.

A 64 oz bottle of Heinz ketchup standing like a sentry. One or two of the fancier mustards unopened.

No one is looking at you.

Eat it.

Eat it all you fat fuck.

Do it.

Your aunts and uncles are all so old. Your parents too. But that provides a kind of cover for you doesn't it?

No one is going to notice if you eat the charcoal meat. Two of them even.

God the beers in the cooler look ice cold. Who would it hurt to drink three to five of them right now?

You could just say you were tired if anyone asked.

Had had a long week.

You're invisible after all. Not old enough that the kids have come to the realization that they better ask you questions about your life for the first time ever before it's too late and not young enough that everything you do is being recorded at all times. So that none of it will ever be forgotten.

Across the yard all of the children were zooming around like low altitude dog-fighting airplanes. Squealing without fear. Fearful of the wrong things rather.

Eternity

Suddenly temperate northeast summer evenings like this one right now do not have value without a week of 95 degree humidity before them.

Much like they say life has no meaning without the counterweight of oblivion.

I would take the meaninglessness of breezy and 70s every day though if it were offered. Throw in the immortality combo pack too. Why not? I could live for a long time inside of that. Watching everyone else pass while I stayed cool and dry. Never breaking a sweat. Not once. Eventually not remembering what or who had been real before. Carrying around a light hoodie just in case for five hundred years. Waiting for a chill that never comes. Not even after I had long since changed my mind.

Red violet, violet red, brick red, magenta

The birds had come back. Unannounced by the way. Uninvited. And with little having been done to the feeder these past few years in terms of upkeep. No point to it of late on my behalf considering their initial absconding.

So here they perched in their chattering dozens picking right back up where they had left off like nothing was amiss.

Like they'd simply stepped out for a smoke and had bumped into a complicated ex in front of the bar and would have to text us later about it but it was basically fine.

Presently the shitting birds taking in the scenery which largely amounted to yours truly and the idiot mutt over there digging for only Christ Himself knows what. Whatever must have died and been buried beneath our poor tortured hydrangea. Or was now being born down there and digging in the opposite direction upward toward an unspoken meeting point.

Nine or ten chipmunks and their associates gawking at us all in the tableau to boot.

The subterranean society these woodland characters have managed to excavate. Teleporting in and out of sight instantly if I so much as breathe weird.

Tunnels like wormholes. Both kinds.

These vomiting birds with the staring problem remain the headline though.

Like lunch-goers on a sidewalk patio watching the pedestrians amble by. People perhaps on their way to a boutique of some renown. To a used record shop that doesn't exist anymore. That you always wondered how it had survived as long as it did come to think of it.

On a nice broad avenue. A series of blocks where the city allows trees to flourish still. Expends resources toward that still. Where bright orange bouquets of hundreds of dollars worth of parking tickets bloom on the windshields of cars that are expensive enough that nothing that could ever happen to them would really matter to the owner.

You've seen this right?

Starched white tablecloths and the plopping of fresh sliced chunks of lemon into tall glasses of sparkling water with the little tongs.

One relatively sicker person from each party ordering a third day-drink and everyone struggling not to remark on it aloud but nonetheless cataloging the fact of it individually and collectively in the subsequent silence.

Maybe saving it for later if it proves necessary as far as character assassination.

For the waitress the question of the fluctuating tip broadcast on the diners' reddening faces like a stock market read out. A formula that only a servant can translate in real time but has to pretend not to be able to.

Then came an alert from the governor on my device saying to be on the lookout for Perverts around every corner and noticing my neighbor Raymond fussing over his truck and receiving this very alert on his phone simultaneously I did the haha I got it too wave with my phone and he started to limp directionally me-wise so now here was this guy in his war veteran baseball cap.

To postpone his tedious interrogation I did the little joke I do every time the governor sends this same alert. Looking around the corners and in the recycling bin and so forth. I grabbed an invisible hatchet and did a whole pantomime about chasing the Perverts out of the yard and Raymond chuckled.

Kill them all he shouted despite being close enough to not need to.

Yes yes kill the Perverts right now in front of God I said.

Just performing it though. You understand.

The variegation in their coloring this cycle Raymond said gesturing with his wrench and pointing toward the tree-full of you know who.

Birds not Perverts that is.

I'd like to get a peek at what's going on inside of there he said. Under the hood so to speak he said. How certain meteorological contrivances have been at play these years he said.

I hated to hand it to Raymond if it wasn't necessary under normal circumstances but these awful birds were in fact beautiful. Reflecting an uncanny light off their disgusting mite-infested feathers. Or I don't know maybe the mites hadn't arrived yet. Maybe this was a brief pocket of unmolested purity for their skin.

Some of them exploding into the second story windows of my home again and again like boomerangs.

You wouldn't want to look too closely under there though I said. With what they might be carrying.

Ah well that's fair enough to say Raymond said gesturing outward toward everything. Indicting the entire expanse of the world.

That being over for now I started to make my way back inside. The co-pilots flicking switches overhead and checking certain meter levels inside of my joints. Come on baby girl I said to the dog. Come on baby idiot I said then felt badly about it and when she didn't look up from her delving I humped over to jag at her choker and felt badly about that too but before long we were safely ensconced inside albeit now at odds temperamentally and meanwhile finding my poor sister resting under an avalanche of pillows. She murmured from within the fort at the sound of our approach. Who is it now she said. I placed my palm on the meat of her and said what is it dear and she said no no no it's not you.

There's a bear chasing me in my dreams she said and so I turned my hand backways onto the skin of her skull which was roiling and I told her that there are no bears anymore.

None of this is real dear sister I said and it was unclear at first if she understood me but she subsequently tucked her head into the blanket of her bicep and after a moment's silence opened her purple eyes and instructed me that I personally do not know what it is that is real and what it is that is not real.

I felt that that was a fair admonition.

I stole her phone from under her couch-smushed cheek to aid in her comfort and glanced at it in the movement and on the screen there was a photo of a robust healthy tree growing toward God's light and in the embrace of its sturdy arm branches was a much skinnier but still flowering tree without a base or roots of any kind. It looked like it had been chainsawed from below long ago and was now suspended in mid-air. Like you'd hold a child up in a pool to prevent its drowning. The larger one nourishing the smaller horizontally in the trick of this levitation.

I went to the water and brought her a glass full and considered myself the brother of the year for that kindness. A kind of benevolent tree you might say. I said I was going to go back outside again and figure out what was to be done at last about the prodigal birds and she lifted herself up on one elbow and squinted at me violet and quivering and said you are going to leave me alone in this world aren't you?

I didn't have an answer for that at first.

That was the kind of accusation you had to turn around and look at from various angles.

To bring math into.

Like how the engineers who design the missiles have to pretend not to know where they're destined to explode.

Yes I said.

Thought that is.

I didn't actually say yes.

Yes I thought though.

But not yet.

No I'm not I said.

I will never leave you alone in this world I said.

The muted TV was looping a montage of colleagues of ours from hither and yon with their chubby little chunk of bright red babies and birdless yards and well-behaved dogs and I gestured to our lazing one and said look at that. Do you see that? This is what I've been trying to tell you I said but she didn't understand me. That being a major source of the building tension between us. The prison of her dog brain. Also the prison of mine. No progress closing the gap on that despite all of everything else moving so rapidly these years.

All of that amounted to a certain degree of blueness in my core roughly a 7 out of 10 in blueness but I breathed in big bales of house oxygen until it was all stabilized and my blood pumped safely and went to check on the status of the birds I mentioned earlier. Here they came again assembling a more concise jury. The bulk of them still nipping and lollygagging and playing around in the trees. Disturbing certain yard improvements I had been working on as far as beautification. There was Raymond too within spitting distance. Still agitated about the sex pests in our midst I wagered.

Somewhere in the neighborhood a drummer was practicing solid snare thwacks like a heartbeat.

Then like an unspooling machine gun.

Let me ask you a question briefly if you don't mind Raymond said. Do you have a staircase in your home that makes you just a little uneasy to walk down?

Not that steep at first but looking steeper of late than it ever had cause to appear previously I mean. Kind of a toothsome beckoning at the foot of it type of thing.

All around us the drummer going duguhdugu hduguhduguh. Killing everyone with his striking. Heaving waves of freshly shaved boys in their little war helmets into a burning hole.

You remember this right?

I guess sometimes I do I said. Consider the stairs from a certain angle.

I mostly live on the first floor now Raymond said. So I'm not confronting the stairs as much as I once might have had to he said.

Just be careful he said and I said that I would.

Do you have a chef's knife in your home that makes you just a little uneasy to use?

I'm not asking Raymond I'm asking you.

Even if it's not as sharp as it once was anymore because who knows how to have knives sharpened at this stage of the game. It would be like having a shoe cobbled. Taking a hat to the milliner. Better to just pitch everything into the dirt hole and then none of it is your problem anymore.

Nothing is your problem anymore.

What about that?

Rotate it around.

A floating 3D text cube of:

Nothing is your problem anymore!

Without an exclamation point actually. Make a note to take the exclamation point out.

What else?

What else.

I thought I might try not being so angry all of the time. Try once again to do that.

Is there no beauty to be found in these birds despite their persistent molestations?

Maybe I should try cataloging the bounty of their colors.

I fetched a notebook and sat and observed quietly and wrote down every hue I recognized from the famously large box of crayons from my youth.

Burnt umber…

…orchid, lavender, carnation pink, thistle, red violet, violet red, brick red, magenta, maroon, mulberry, indian red, melon, salmon, orange red, red orange, flesh...

The thing about birds is that alongside all of their elaborate plumage they have another devilish adaptation which is that they can see colors that we cannot. Ultraviolet frequencies for example. More colors than they're even capable of growing for themselves.

A hawk perceiving a faint trail of rodent urine from the sky.

An insect announcing its whereabouts like the flickering of a motel's signage.

The seeds of a plant confessing their desire to be carried off elsewhere to propagate their lineage forward.

To be carried literally anywhere else but here.

...maize, goldenrod, yellow orange, apricot, orange yellow, lemon yellow, green yellow, spring green, yellow green, sea green, olive green...

And what that we think we've kept hidden can they see of us? What barely visible aura of ours do we broadcast for them as we tumble so slowly down the steeper and steeper stairs?

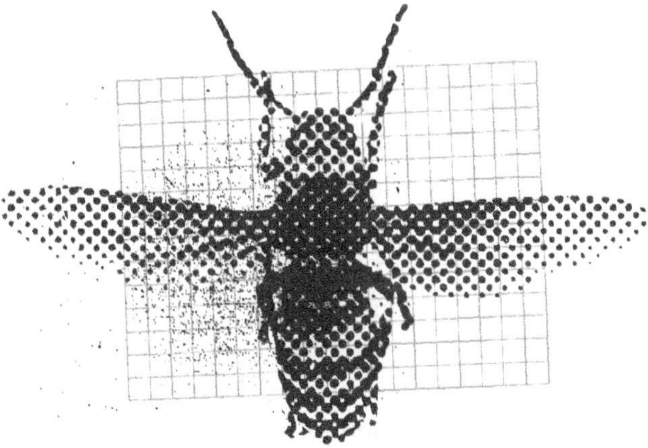

Look now look again

I watched a video of a man being burned alive in a hospital tent. The IV still attached to his flailing arm.

Someone was trying to heal him and someone was trying to harm him and the latter won out in that contest as they almost always do. Murder being so much quicker and easier than medicine.

I didn't actually watch the video. I lied and I'm sorry about that. I watched maybe five seconds of it before I had to look away.

How easy that is to do right?

I couldn't bring myself to watch the whole thing. I don't know if he would have wanted us to watch it. Some of us would want that if it were us and some of us would not. I suppose I would if I thought it was going to make a single fucking difference but no picture or video has made a single fucking difference over this past year of slaughter. No matter how horrific the images of suffering captured on film day after day of man woman child or infant being crushed or burned or assassinated by bullet there will always be someone saying that they deserved it. Often most of our elected officials and the majority of the media. More typically some random regular person. I don't think I have ever read about or watched the death of a civilian during this genocide without someone saying in the comments that they had it coming.

I did watch the video from a few months ago of the young man asking for help from anyone who might be watching. Trying to explain his predicament. He was the provider for his family because he is the oldest he said. He had two sisters and two little brothers and his parents to take care of he said. He was studying software engineering he said.

After that I saw a picture of an ice cream refrigerator with a neat stack of tiny bodies packed into it. Wrapped in the white cloth shrouds that have become such a familiar sight all year.

"Here is the children's favorite ice cream fridge being their morgue in Gaza," a Palestinian journalist posted.

I just looked at her bio.

"Both a human rights activist and journalist, what's the difference anyway?" it reads.

That is right. I believe that. That is what the job is. Or is supposed to be.

Don't worry though my friend. Help is perchance coming. Not today no. Not a few days ago when you were still alive. Not one year ago or ten. Maybe if certain things go well just after the next election they might take action to save you. You who have already been burned.

Control control control control
control control control

I had been sick for a couple of days feverish and chilled and incapable of experiencing joy although that third one wasn't exactly new for me. I took a Covid test that came up negative and not long after was like oh right. I experienced the very dumb epiphany that a person can just at any time for no reason become ill in the very standard manner that had fallen out of fashion there for a few years.

On the morning of Thanksgiving it was negotiated that I would stay home instead of heading down to the shore to dine with my in-laws and I felt something like loss mingled with excitement at least in part on account of the potential Kevin McCallister scenarios.

More than any of that though I felt relieved of a burden considering how eating-based holidays like this are a driver of exceptional dread for people like me.

Every holiday is eating-based I suppose but this is the big one. The Super Bowl of binging. The normal Super Bowl is also the Super Bowl of binging but you follow me.

So instead of feeling morose that I'd be spending the first Thanksgiving of my entire life alone it felt like a reprieve in that I would not have to eat and eat and eat right there in front of my wife's cousins and God and everyone.

One doesn't have to but one does anyway you know? How you drink more deeply and lustily when there's an open bar. It costs something sure but it's nonetheless free.

Then when that brief high wore off later I remembered that I would have to at least eat a little bite of something at some point and that we didn't have anything in the house besides expiring vindaloo. On top of the lack of food if I'm honest was the absence of anything to drink which was an amateur mistake on my behalf in terms of preparedness. One of the first things they teach you as a New England townie is which days the package stores are closed on account of the Puritans' centuries old shame.

Also how you can't buy scratchies with a debit card. That one was a good call at least.

After a couple hours of football-based sloth I walked up to the packy and thought I'd buy some of the disgusting holiday flavored Polar soda waters they have out now and then sneak a six pack into the transaction like a nervous teenager disguising his condoms but they clocked me instantly and rudely to be frank. It was as if they saw me coming a mile away.

Then it was like now what.

I went home and drank my Pomegranate Champagne Soda and started calling around figuring maybe the Chinese places in the area would be open and then worried I was racist for thinking that.

Eventually in my research I saw that this Frank Sinatra-ass suburban golf dad steakhouse with the $60 filet and the $20 green beans was open and so feeling somewhat better now health- and outlook-wise I drove twenty minutes over there along the stretch through the desiccating marshes and found a seat at the bar next to a fifty something couple that looked drunk enough to be planning on fucking each other when they got home but also drunk enough that they might be too drunk to follow through with it by the time they got there. Drunk enough too that they were one hundred percent going to break a glass before they left.

I ordered a Negroni that came out at roughly a half a pint and drank from its medicine and all of a sudden I wasn't sick anymore. It was a holiday miracle. A very bad lesson for me to learn.

I asked them to bring me a plate of Rhode Island style calamari that arrived soon with the hot peppers and the marinara and the half of a lemon inside of the mesh places like this give you so you can squeeze it all over and I poked my fork around the dish to give the gin at least something to contend with inside of my guts.

It was unclear to me if I was underdressed here. Half the people were millionaires and half were going to be dead within two years and looked like it so I didn't need to impress them.

I looked at my phone and read a thread pushing back against the suddenly commonplace idea that queer people and the left are all groomers.

It went on for a while but the salient point for me was about conservatives throughout history "...systematically lying about groups people are already socially authorized to dislike..."

That's a sentence that put some things I've been thinking about into focus. It has for every single day that I've been alive been socially acceptable to either mock or villainize or place a target on the heads of people who are simply agitating for a more equitable and less predatory organization of society.

Even expressing such a wish for a better world has always been seen as de facto comical. The musings of a hybrid goofy romantic or would-be authoritarian in the way that the right always characterizes their enemies as both weak and all-powerful at once.

Then I had some of the newly presented cup of corn chowder that was thicker than crude oil and must have been two thousand calories per spoonful and hated myself for it and I read another tweet that went something like:

"In America, victims of mass shootings aren't even guaranteed thoughts and prayers anymore."

That seemed profound to me but now a couple days later thinking about it again I don't think it's true. I think the thoughts and prayers are still proffered it's just that the right has given up on the pretense of lying about the specific content of those thoughts and prayers.

You can speak clearly about what you believe and want to happen to your political enemies when you are on the right in America but you cannot do so from the left. You have to be cute about it. Always thus but even more so now.

I thought back to a conversation I had with a friend a couple years ago on the case for the left arming themselves.

"In a lot of this discussion around arming the left it's not an offensive posture, it's a defensive one. For example, if twenty of us showed up trying to scrap with the cops, that's twenty funerals. It's stupid. But if we're at a protest and twenty of us are there open-carrying, not causing any issues, just establishing a presence, the cops are going to act differently when they try to come toward the protestors we're trying to protect."

I am not going to get a gun to be clear. Only in part because of shit like this study I read that said "people who live with handgun owners are shot to death at a higher rate than those who don't have such weapons at home."

"We found zero evidence of any kind of protective effects" from living in a home with a handgun the Stanford researcher said.

After that I read some of a story about how tumultuous the Colorado Springs shooter's childhood was and thought hmm me too but I just got into comic books and loud music and sports instead of going out and killing everyone.

Just now I went and looked back at notes I took during a conversation with my mother a few months ago so I could answer some questions my therapist had about my childhood. This part stood out:

"He sat there with a gun to your head. I don't know how much you remember. But you lived in a trauma filled world. He never physically abused you. He was abusive to me. But as a result our household was full of trauma. He was gone shortly after the episode with the gun but continued to terrorize our home. Burned down the guest house. Police constantly coming by. Does a two year old absorb that? Maybe?"

Maybe!

There was a crash and a squeal and sure enough the couple next to me had broken a martini glass. The biggest hunk was jutting out of the sopping bar mats like a jagged rock formation. The type of thing you could kill yourself on if you weren't careful. The veteran bartender in his vest and bowtie who was visibly desperate for his shift to be over said don't touch it I'll do it.

Do not touch it he said again sternly but kindly and then they paid and left and drove home drunk to wherever it is these people drive home to. Lincoln, Massachusetts probably. Wayland perhaps. Weston.

I guess we'll never know if they ended up boning or not.

I drunk drove home myself not long after and realized I was missing my own family at this point. All of my family. Family I wasn't even meant to have seen one way or another today. I read a bunch of the typical posts about Thanksgiving Uncles and it dawned on me that I was lucky to never really have that kind of uncle. All me and my uncles ever really talk about is how insane my grandmother made us all and how cool it was to go see Santana all the time in the seventies.

I posted something to that effect when I got home and someone shared a video of Santana playing Soul Sacrifice at Woodstock and it just consumed me for the next hour.

Everyone in the band is five seconds away from collapsing but just so in the pocket and on the moon at the same time.

I read a YouTube comment:

"The whole band is battling quantum realities but the drummer is keeping the portal open."

I looked back again at the notes from the talk with my mother.

"It was from an early age. The last time you were comfortable in your body was maybe 12."

Somewhere around my seventh watch through the Santana video my wife arrived home bearing plates of Thanksgiving leftovers and I thought nooo I was so close to pulling off calorie deficit Thanksgiving. I would have gotten away with it if it weren't for the stupid stubborn care of my loved ones.

I had this pointless daydream about not eating any of it. I pictured myself going to bed not having microwaved an overflowing plate of stuffing and bird drenched in gravy and potatoes and squash and green beans and roll after roll and it was such a nice little fantasy to live inside of for a little while. To imagine myself the type of person who wouldn't have to do that. What it must feel like to be in control of something. Even if it's only your own body.

The hunger

Well we just got back from stringing up our weakest friend in the middle of the town square for the vampires to feast on overnight. No one liked the actual doing of it when it came to doing it I'll say that. But the past is the past. Time now to hunker down inside and wait for them to leave us alone for good. Figure out tomorrow what to do with all these surplus wooden crosses.

How to throw your life away

My childhood bedroom is so very small. It feels as if the walls are closing in. Part of that might be the way that everything in the home you grew up in seems smaller when you come back to it as an adult but it's also probably because when the house was built a few hundred years ago people didn't have as many useless possessions to hold onto forever as we do now.

There's a big rock out back with a plaque on it to commemorate the historic significance of the area but I forget most of the details now.

They were born and then they lived and then they died as the song goes.

I used to climb onto the rock when I was young and unbothered by history and look out at the farm next door that had a total of one horse and one cow. It always seemed like the loneliest farm in the world to me but maybe it was just an exceptionally efficient one.

Every year around the start of spring I get a call from my mother asking me to come contend with the entire history of my youth which has been abandoned in this room for almost twenty years. It's like the persistent alerts you get on your phone saying you're running out of photo space and it's time to upgrade your storage but even phones don't yet have the power to guilt you into action like mothers do.

This year I finally gave in.

Inside the bedroom was a mess. Box after box filled with the detritus of my past. There were old comic books my mother insisted must be worth some money and projects dating back to elementary school and high school and college essays. There were some morbid poems written in an unrecognizable scrawl that I'd bound together into a book with a flowery wallpaper covering. I must have recently read Emily Dickinson's Because I Could Not Stop for Death for the first time when I made it because one verse was clearly a rip-off.

I found a treasure trove of cassette tapes as well including some I'd even listen to right now—Dinosaur Jr., Liz Phair, Alice in Chains—and some like a Hootie & the Blowfish live bootleg from 1992. I don't know what to tell you man the 90s were weird.

Then postcards from girls I no longer remember and long desperate letters from ones I always will. I would not like to read now how I responded if I did.

Pictures of friends whose names are lost to me and pictures of friends who I still see all the time and posters of concerts I'd been to by bands that haven't existed in decades. There were Boy Scout badges and photos of me and my friends looking like we were in a 90s boy band and photos of my dead friend who actually was in a 90s boy band and photos of people I'd thought at the time would be in my life forever and of course would not.

I found my old shit in other words which feels like an appropriate term because I thought it all surprisingly foul.

A high school friend came to visit me recently. There was a mixtape he had made for me in the room. He wanted to show me his latest project. It was thousands of archived emails that our group of friends had sent each other beginning in 1996. At first I was thrilled about the prospect of being able to read what we were talking about back then but the excitement didn't last long. Here was someone writing under my name in a voice that no longer exists and what was worse speaking at length and with no shortage of emotional conviction about things I no longer remember ever caring about. I felt the same way about the dusty boxes of memories. A strange dissociative feeling like none of this had ever happened or had happened to someone else. Someone who wasn't me. Reading some of my old letters and emails felt like eavesdropping on conversations that I wasn't meant to hear or at least that my clearance level should have been revoked for by now.

It all engendered something like a sense of revulsion.

Throw it all away I told my mother later. I don't want any of it. It's not mine I said. Which hurt her feelings. That's something I seem to be very good at doing.

It's supposed to be hard for people to let go of their sentimental clutter from what I understand. But the more I looked at these things the less real the memories actually felt.

People keep stuff for all kinds of reasons. Some do it because they feel loyalty to the person who gave it to them and think throwing the item away would be a sort of betrayal. I have had a number of old letters my grandmother sent me stashed away for over a decade now because disposing of them would feel like desecrating her grave in a way.

Maybe other people feel that getting rid of something would be a break from the past that they don't want to go through with?

It's not that the inherent value of an item has changed over time but rather that we ourselves have changed.

A week or two later I called my mother back to ask her if she'd thrown everything away yet. There are a few more things I want to keep I said. I needed to come back to take another pass at editing down my story. I'd already taken some photo albums with me and a scant few books including the Dickinson which I am definitely going to get around to reading again.

My mother is a quilter. When someone dies his or her family will bring leftover t-shirts and sweaters to her to stitch together into a blanket that they can wrap themselves in. It's weaving together the literal fabric of a life. Oftentimes there's simply too much material so decisions must be made. It's similar to how we have to deal with our own lives as we go along. You can't hold every memory in your head at once it would be maddening. Instead we pick and choose which ones to keep sometimes subconsciously or sometimes by deciding that a certain day or a certain interaction or a certain smell or a handful of objects among hundreds will be the ones we think we will want to remember forever. And then we put the rest in a little box somewhere and bury it. And then one day we crawl into the box too.

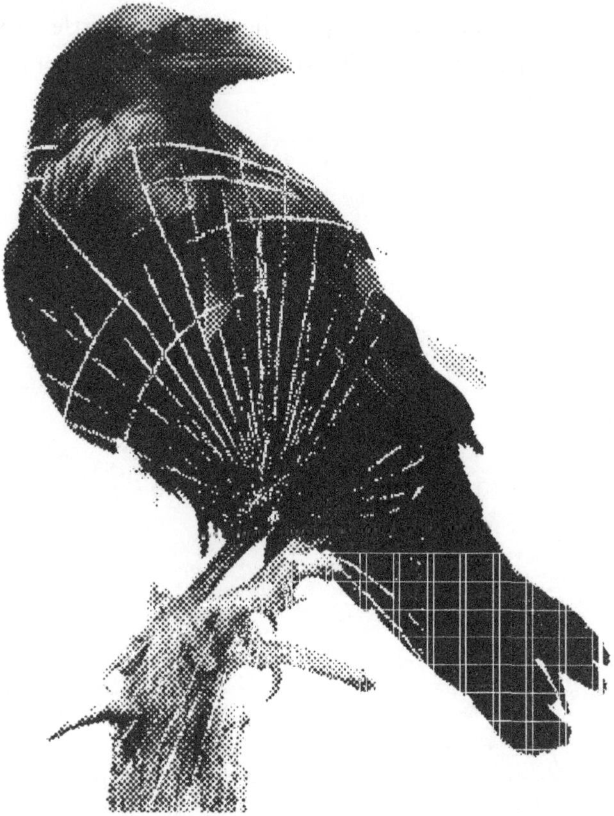

I love you so much when you are asleep

My football anxiety was filling the room like poison gas so you went upstairs to read by which you meant look at TikTok and after the game when I was spreading and straightening the blanket out over you to arrange everything perfectly before I died I accidentally sprung your glasses off onto the floor somewhere.

I looked for them for so long while you slept soundly. So you would have them there for you when you needed to see the morning. I crawled around on all fours in the slim moonlight and conked my head on the bed frame. They'd have put a replay of my dumb ass online if we had had one of those night vision cameras for spotting ghosts in the bedroom.

I just wanted you to know about that. I know that I am still alive right now and will hopefully be for a good long while but this was technically speaking before I died. Maybe you won't read this until after I don't know. How many thousands of other little things like that do we both do for each other that we keep to ourselves? Someone should write a book.

After the wind

After the wind had abated they drove east on a length of flat empty plains highway hoping to outstrip its inevitable redoubling and were silent for some miles before the first of the overturned tractor trailers on the shoulder appeared and then the next and the next and the next passing almost evenly spaced out now like mile markers. The symmetry of the trucks' resting was mystifying. Never mind the simple fact of their all toppling like so.

It all unfolded like that for a while. Less like the aftermath of a cyclone's tantrum than a formal laying down of arms by a retreating army.

Or a herd of animals showing its collective belly.

More peaceful than that.

Horses slumbering in an orderly and well kept stable.

They kind of remind me of horses sleeping she said and he said don't horses sleep standing up and she said not when they are actually sleeping. In deep sleep I mean. In REM sleep. They have to lie down for that.

When did you ever see a horse sleeping he said and she said we had a horse when I was young and he said what was it called and she hesitated and said I don't remember it's name but she sounded like a liar buying time.

Her phone wasn't working correctly so the screen was stuck on the last article she had tried to open from before. It was a tabloid she hate-read. Archaeologists uncover Egyptian mummies with golden tongues it said. That phrasing wormed into her pulse compounding its musicality with each swipe down on the screen when it would not disappear upon a refresh.

Schwip.

Mummies with golden tongues.

Schwip.

Mummies with golden tongues.

Ancient tombs containing corpses with precious metals in mouths the subhead read.

Schwip.

Precious metals in mouths.

The full article never ended up loading so she didn't get to read through to see what it said. Apparently they used to remove the deceased's tongue and replace it with a hunk of gold so they would have an offering on hand when it came time to speak to Osiris the judge of the dead. How reasoning is always less effective than a bribe in an audience with the powerful.

The razor

Washing up prior to toppling over into an empty and unmade bed and out of nowhere I could feel a hair growing out of my temple.

I could hear it too almost. Its sprouting.

This is the kind of thing that happens backstage every microsecond of every day for every mammal that has ever existed but somehow I had caught it in flagrante delicto. When it must have assumed I would have had my defenses down.

Coming home early from a business trip to a big surprise from your spouse.

It sort of hurt on top of it all. My hair had never hurt me before now. It was as if a new tooth was coming in on the side of my skull. Or watching a pimple form in real time.

Or a scar healing. Which was also happening inside of me so much slower than I needed it to.

I'd only just learned the other day that our ears get bigger as we age.

The human body is a prison with only the one exit but at least they made it minimum security. And the guards are always asleep.

A nightmare I plan on having

Conan O'Brien was looming over me and stabbing his pointed finger downward into my chest. He really is quite tall like they say. You piece of shit he said spittling about the mouth. You'll never amount to anything he said. I'll see to that he said. His face was pomegranate purple and his eyes had rolled into the back of his head. I was about two seconds away from breaking down and bawling right there on the sidewalk in front of a large crowd that had gathered. People said later that it was the first time they had ever seen him in public not doing shtick.

He spit on the ground and started back toward his waiting car and turned before getting in.

And your sad little poems suck too he said.

Wait I said. Mr. O'Brien sir.

Have you really read my books?

Bowels

The girl in the pink pajama bottoms was writhing in anguish splayed out across three waiting room chairs which probably isn't out of the ordinary for an emergency department but he thought perhaps naively that someone would be arriving sooner than this to help her. To collect her up. Swaddle her. At least usher her backstage. Certainly they can't let this play out in front of the customers he thought. The patients.

You might briefly believe that's how it works then you remember. Sometimes you just get left somewhere. Sometimes you collapse just before the finish line.

I can't do it she said. I can't do it. Over and over. I can't do it. Punctuated only by a brief moment of heroic resolve when she would say I can do it. I can do it. One gasp of hope out of twenty resignations.

It was some kind of withdrawal situation he presumed having been through a similar routine a number of times himself over the years. More often than not on the floor of his bedroom or bathroom twisting and twisting like a man rolling down a hill but not going anywhere. Praying and praying and punching himself in the face out of some deluded and desperate plan to bring on merciful temporary silence. Eternal maybe. Who cares. Just not this.

He sat there on the morning of Memorial Day unclear of the etiquette in these sorts of situations with a few elderly couples waiting for their version of pain to be addressed on the record and he thought about how much better he was going to feel when some professional arrived and appraised his own suffering. Gave him a thorough once over. When they look you up and down and say it's not as bad as you were worried that it was going to be.

The relief of that.

How stupid we all are.

She had her hoodie pulled up over her head so he couldn't tell how old she was. He thought middle aged but the pajamas made her seem so much younger. It's confounding because addiction makes you old beyond your years over time but also often renders you an infant in the interim.

You can do it he said sort of under his breath as she puked into a blue plastic bag they must have given her earlier. You can do it uh ma'am. But he knew that was nothing to her. Is nothing to anyone.

You can do it.

That doesn't help anyone.

He didn't think she could do it to be honest.

He got a text that said the Democrats were having some kind of big 700% donation matching deal going on and he thought wow I had better not pass up on this opportunity while it's hot. He texted his girlfriend that it didn't seem that busy all things considered what with the holiday so they'd probably come take care of him soon he said.

I can't do it the woman said and he looked around and all of the nurses were going about their normal routine. He thought they would know better than him when something really bad is happening. That's basically their entire job.

A big sign broadcasting triage over one of the desks.

When there's turbulence and you look at the flight attendants and they're still dicking around on their phones and chatting back there so you know you're not going to die this time.

I can't do it.

He thought that he couldn't do it personally if it came down to it. Any of this. He can but he could not. Not sure for how much longer though either way.

So then they called him in and he jogged up like he was on a game show and explained standing there with his weight belt on that his guts were absolutely fucked. But the thing was he didn't know if it was a drinking every day scenario or lifting weights every day scenario and the meat of the matter was that he couldn't sit down without severe discomfort in his lower abdomen and also it was painful to you know what. No the other one. The nice one. Out of nowhere he had developed a pot belly he said. A distended abdomen he said he thought it was called.

They put him in a bed and hooked him up to the machines and sucked out his blood through the tubes and the piss through his penis and long story short they did all the images and tests and were ultimately like well uh it's nothing bad that we can see. Probably just a pulled muscle.

They were all very nice and professional about it he thought but after all just sent him back out on his way to deal with it on his own. To deal with everything.

Maybe cut back on the drinking though they said and he had two different answers for that.

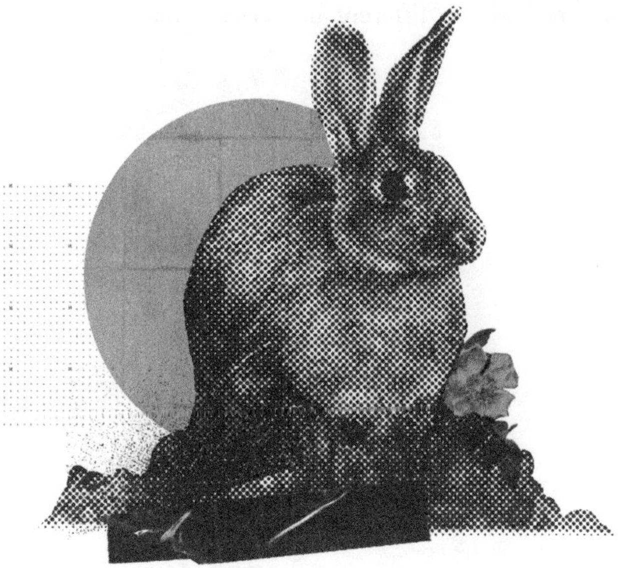

Nothing could go wrong

I was in the middle of apologizing for barking at you to please stop singing Linger by the Cranberries over and over and over while you were washing the dishes when there was a horrific screeching and then a violent thud outside at the intersection. Like one of their missiles had found us. No one crying out though. The subsequent silence almost as scary. We both leapt up to look out the window and saw two mangled cars embracing one another. A freeze frame of a goal line tackle. The neighbors all skittered out onto the street toward the crash and the braver among them were trying to pry open the doors and break through the windows. We got there a moment later and were standing in the back of the scrum when I spotted him coming around the corner getting closer and closer and closer and the only thing I could think of to do to help was pick up a rock and chuck it at his head. I swear to Christ man I beaned him right in the dome. Throwing 93 it felt like. Sliding up and to the right. Stopped him dead in his tracks for a moment or two. I'd never been so alive before. I felt like Pedro Martinez.

He kept coming anyway though which was pretty deflating. Collected the drivers up in short order in his sack. But what a high it had briefly been. I worried that he was going to remember it. Take me yard next time. Maybe charge the mound.

After I asked you to sing me the Cranberries song again and you did even though I could tell you really didn't have the spark in you anymore. Had forgotten some of the lyrics.

Whatever it is that's swimming down there

Indigenous people in Alaska and other northern regions have been hunting whales for thousands of years which sounds almost impossible doesn't it. I can barely reconcile the fact that whales even exist today never mind think about seeing one hundreds or thousands of years ago and saying to myself I am going to eat that. I can't boil rice without my wife having to come in from the other room frowning.

Have you ever been on a whale watching trip and you go out in the little sad boat the guy owns and you sit there for a while like this blows and then you finally see a whale and you're like holy shit are you seeing this shit? Your entire life changes right there next to some guy from Arizona.

Holy fucking shit.

Now imagine you're a guy in a much shittier boat from a thousand years ago and you gotta go fight the whale. Where would you even start?

I suppose if you are very hungry there are no limits to the ingenuity of man. There are also no limits to the greed of man which is why we aren't allowed to hunt whales anymore. We got so good at killing them and making money off of it we almost ruined them and everything forever.

Bowhead whales for example were almost wiped out by commercial whaling from 1848 to 1915 which brought the population of the species down to around one thousand worldwide. Scientists estimate there are about fourteen thousand of them swimming around down there now oblivious to our bullshit so that is good. Until we boil them later.

On one particular whaling expedition in 2007 Inupiat hunters in Alaska pulled in a fifty-ton bowhead somehow and after digging deep through the layers and layers of blubber they found something curious which was a harpoon lodged in its shoulder bone. The weapon was dated to the late 1800s and the experts said it was a type of exploding lance produced in New Bedford when it was the whaling capital of the world and long before I used to have to ride on a bus down there in high school to go get my head stomped in playing football.

Whalers in those days would fire the harpoon from a shoulder-held device and it would shoot out and chunk into the whale and then explode inside of the whale and it would kill the whale if all went well. Sometimes in other cases like this one the whale would say fuck you and go swim off to live the rest of its whale life in peace while the guy on the boat maybe thought ahhhh I'm ruined and then would starve to death or go to jail for his debts. However people got fucked over back then. Same as now I suppose.

The fact that this whale had lived so long with a century-old weapon inside of its bones was revealing because while scientists have long estimated that whales could live for a very long time they didn't know it was that long. This one had lived for at least one hundred and fifteen years meaning as far as they could speculate the idea that whales could live up to two hundred years wasn't out of the question anymore.

Can you imagine living that long with a harpoon lodged inside of your body? Even living that long in the first place? Two hundred years. That means there are maybe whales swimming around out there right now that were born before Moby Dick was written. Some of them still meaning to finally finish reading it when they have some free time.

Traditionally the way scientists determine the age of a whale is by studying the amino acids in its eyes. Another weird thing about bowhead whales is that they tend not to develop cancer which is very surprising considering the vast number of cells they have. Cancer absolutely loves cells. Cancer cannot get enough of that shit.

Scientists who have sequenced their genome are hoping to figure out how to apply that sort of thing to humans to help prevent aging-related diseases which sounds pretty cool until you think again about the idea of living for two hundred years. I've lived barely a quarter of that and I've already almost seen enough. The way we've treated whales for one example. Everything else also.

Research into all that is being funded in part by a group called the Methuselah Foundation whose mission is "to make 90 the new 50 by 2030." After poking around their website they look like the type of corporation who end up accidentally inventing vampires in a video game.

Methuselah was the oldest dude in the Bible and Noah's grandfather. The Bible says he lived nine hundred and sixty-nine years before dying in the flood we all know about.

It would be a pretty grim irony if humans finally figured out how to live to one hundred and fifty and then we all died in the other flood that's coming and it didn't end up mattering after all.

There's a bunny I see out in my backyard all the time and since I was reading about whale lifespans I just looked up how long they live in the wild and the computer said one or two years which isn't very long at all. Domesticated ones can live around nine years but it's admittedly a bit of a tradeoff for them freedom-wise.

I saw some fresh tracks in the snow this morning and I was thinking about how cool it would be to be able to jump as far as they do. Not cool enough to be worth dying after like fifteen months but still pretty cool you have to admit.

I'd jump so much if I could.

I was standing under a basketball net inside of a gymnasium recently when I went to vote and change the world via my single responsibility under democracy and thinking about how pathetic it would look if I tried to jump up and grab the rim which is something I unimaginably could actually do at one point in my life.

Never dunk though. I could have easily lied about having been able to do that here but a man's integrity is all he has in the end.

When was the last time you jumped?

Really jumped I mean.

Some day will be the last day you ever jump and you won't know it and then you'll never jump again. You'll live the rest of your life planted firmly on the ground and getting closer and closer to being inside of it with every passing minute.

The Red Line

I was outside the Burger King at Park Street keeping my head down but not all that much more tense than I would have usually been around here when the State House dome collapsed. From a previous thing I think. Nothing hot at the moment. Just all of the supports finally giving in. Like an elephant falling down.

They had flown back down again and gotten our asses pretty quickly. So now we were on the other end of that. Not as bad as you would have thought it would be for everyone everywhere all at once mind you. Just kind of a gradual expansion. Like when the Tatte bakeries started popping up on every block. Like viscous spilled oil. You could run away from it for the time being. Which is what I was just doing a minute ago.

I turned right on Bromfield Street and I had the instinctual thought to duck into Silvertone for a quick one but they were boarded up. Had been since even before all of this it looked like. Everything was fucked one way or the other. I would have joked that the world was ending if I had heard about them closing a year or two ago.

Something rumbling over at the Granary Burying Ground by Park Street Church. A memory from a childhood Freedom Trail tour of thousands of bodies buried there. The Infant's Tomb. John Hancock. Paul Revere.

Okay now they were shooting laser guns back and forth down on Washington Street by the Marshalls. I only just learned those existed a few days ago. So I pissed myself and ran around the corner thinking to hide in the alley outside of the Orpheum but two hundred people or more were already there trying to break in. Weeping and rending. Like people you used to see on the news from somewhere else where people suffer more routinely. They were going to break in soon it looked like.

I imagined someone inside of there was getting ready to put on a big show. Everyone screaming in their seats. Not a dry eye in the house.

This too not much different than before.

I told myself that lie.

It's not too late

It's hard to lose track of anyone anymore. Before people just came and went in and out of your life and yes that was bad in its own way but a way that doesn't matter anymore. Now we just have to carry around the details of every single life with us forever. Even if we don't particularly want to. A backpack weighted down with souls.

That said we all have good friends of our good friends who we have always liked when we saw them exclusively via the mutual friend as the axis but that we may never have ended up following online and so it's nice to hear what they are up to every few years. Kind of a *previously on...* scenario.

In your twenties it will be about who is getting married or what their job is and in your thirties it's usually about who has had children and where they've moved to and in your forties it's about cataloging who has gotten divorced or else who has gotten sick and who never got better.

I don't know what it's like beyond that. Maybe it gets magically happier out of nowhere!

That's one thing we talked about the other night. How so and so was.

I haven't seen them in forever man. He asked about you. Yeah it was rough but they're doing alright now. They didn't make it.

Almost no one makes it out.

I have a lot of friends who have wisely quit smoking and when they see me they use it as their one little free pass. For old time's sake. Looking around conspiratorially. Making sure their wife isn't paying attention. Like the clumsy drug handshakes we used to do with each other.

I was telling my guys these guys that I need to stop smoking because I really do not want to die which is true believe it or not and one of them said there is still time to stop. It's not too late he said.

Then he bummed one off of me and we stepped outside onto the porch into a light summer rain.

Light enough you could still smoke in it.

He asked if I had ever thought of killing myself.

Not because I was being weird or morose or anything. It was prompted by something or other that came up naturally in our riffing. Maybe someone we used to know had done it for example. Or a musician that we had all collectively loved at one point.

That's what had happened actually. That was what it was.

I said sure I've thought about it but only in the way that everyone does. That I presume everyone does.

Do they he said.

Yes I assume so. What else is there to think about? There is an extremely famous play about this very question. The most famous play and question of all time probably.

He asked if I had ever imagined how I would do it and I said no no no you don't do that. They say if you have a specific plan for how you would do it that that's a real bad sign.

Who said that?

I got in a pickle over that kind of thing once with a nurse and some cops I said.

Then he pressed me and I said alright alright and I told him how I guess I would do it if he really needed to know and he thought about it for a minute or two after I was done and said Jesus Christ dude.

Like he was the one who later finds me.

He said he was going to say that his idea was to cover himself in honey and wait in the woods for a bear to eat him. He said he didn't know we were talking seriously here. He thought we were doing a bit.

Ok fine then I said. I promise I will do it in a silly way if that makes everyone feel better I said.

I'll lay down in front of a very slowly approaching steamroller and pretend I don't see it coming.

I'll rig a pulley to lift a baby grand up into an apartment window and drop it and it will smash down onto my head and my teeth will turn into piano keys.

I'll tuck a napkin into my collar as a bib and open a serving dish I'm expecting to be a succulent ham and then find the stick of dynamite. I'll slice it like a carrot and take a big bite.

I'll write this book and wait for it to sell poorly.

Down the line some of the friends of our friends might wonder what we've been up to. Sneaking outside for a smoke of their own. Just this one they'll lie. Telling ghost stories about so and so.

Whatever happened to ___ one will ask.

Well it's a kind of a funny story.

The ancient thing that it is

I heard that a so-called vigilante was hunting the unhoused with a bow and arrow and then came an alert for a fresh obituary for my long dead aunt on a site I'd never heard of that was apparently AI-scraping newspapers to turn into gibberish and it said at the top that more than anything else my dear aunt loved to be alive and there were nails in the stomachs of the dolphins at an aquarium and I shared an article about a beloved to me band releasing their first album in a decade and someone informed me instantly that as it happens the singer is a transphobe now but those 90 seconds of excitement before that were genuinely so pleasant to be inside of and next they were saying people had been setting up multiple fundraisers to get some people out of the warzone but instead they were stealing the money and getting away with it and Paul Bowles was asking me how many more times do I suppose it will be that I watch the full moon rise and all of my old bartender friends were texting each other about something we didn't want to believe was real and the neighborhood skunk was walking its commute along the same straight path forty five degrees off the end of my porch where it had walked a dozen times or more on some recent nights and my skin tingled in the way it does when something bad but not in the balance of things all that bad was threatening to happen and I gave CVS my phone number to save 60 cents and I gave 7-Eleven my phone number to save 30 cents.

Near Christmas now and two dozen or twenty wild turkeys were loitering in the unsnowed backyard when something in the nearby thicket must have spooked them and they all at once hurled themselves into the sky as far as they could reach and landed in the safety of a white pine perch with their grasping talons. You couldn't have choreographed it more seamlessly. God could but not you. I have never seen turkeys actually fly that high off the ground in my entire life and I've seen a lot of turkeys. Not to boast. Usually just sort of briefly pecking around the sidewalks of Cambridge where I have always wanted to live out the rest of my days so badly but now cannot afford to and probably never could have. Rarely jumping like that though. More so how I would look going up to grab a rebound at this point in my life. Wobbling with a heft and a bottomness to them. Little Godzillas.

Here snuck around the corner next Willow the cat who makes my eyes sting swaggering through the bushes with such confidence. The slim king of all that he surveys. Like a rapper walking into a fake club in a music video. No idea that the thing he wanted most in the world in that moment would have been his undoing which I found relatable.

Inside my mother-in-law was heating dark rum and brown sugar with cloves and citrus.

The turkey had been dismantled.

They take the talons off before we eat them.

People were talking about a famous actress' famous breasts for the third straight week and I wish they would shut the fuck up because a guy can't be going around thinking about that kind of thing all day when he's just trying to mind his own business. With his mother-in-law around.

I think what they were trying to do was to start a fight over the concept of beauty itself. Which group of us it should belong to. Which of us gets to perceive it and which of us do not.

None of us were arguing about the substance of the thing though it's all abstracted out to arguments about how we argue.

Something queer is happening in that my brain is sanding off the bulk of my early memories day by day. Concurrently I'm not replacing those memories with anything of substance. New experiences with any kind of tangible weight to them.

The assistant manager is nodding out in the office and not keeping up with inventory.

How you can sense a store is not long for this world many months before the fact of it is made plain. Admitted to. Of late they are no longer restocking what would intuitively to all seem like a staple of such an establishment. Ah well you know it's the trucks the guy says as an excuse when you ask. To buy time. To put off the inevitable. The warehouses perhaps. Supply chains.

More likely the invoices are simply past due. Each escalating notice impaled on a desk spike in anger. The kind you could put your hand through if you weren't careful.

What about this thing I just thought?

Imagine cropping a photo of yourself on your phone. Pressing on the rectangle icon and then pinching it smaller and smaller each day.

I don't even remember if I've used that analogy before.

You're editing a photo on your phone and you hit the button to rotate it ninety degrees the wrong way and now something that seconds ago was familiar briefly startles you.

You're surprised with the punishment of the front-facing camera but in reverse.

Oh God is that what the world actually looks like?

Is that what everything looks like?

I called home because it was my dad's birthday and then my mother came on the line after some doing to get there and said that her cataract surgery was finally taking hold and then they killed by lethal injection a fifty year old man in Texas whose guilt was doubted by many and as his final words he said "I do not think that this situation here will bring you closure…If this is what it takes…then so be it."

It was reported that the robot dogs were on the ground in Gaza and on the ground at the border in Texas and everyone else was saying yes exactly that is the place where they were always meant to have ended up and Ray Carver was writing about moving toward whatever ancient thing it is that works the chains and pulls us so relentlessly on.

Mothers Day now and I read about women who said they could no longer feed their newborns anymore because they couldn't produce any milk due to the starvation and trauma and the single biggest problem in my life as we speak is that I gained ten pounds that at this age I will likely never lose until I lose a lot of them in a rapid shuddering succession later on and I wonder sometimes why we need to invent alien planets in science fiction because each of us already lives on one of our own and Bernadette Mayer was telling me to work my ass off to change the language and do not ever get famous and that second part seemed very easy to me.

The election was looming and supposedly the fascism at home and abroad was about to get worse if he wins and I think that will be true indeed but we're talking about degrees of fascism now. We're dicing an onion that is gushing blood. Chopping all the way up onto our own fingers in the process without even noticing. We've already long since established what kind of country we are to paraphrase the old joke. Now we're just negotiating.

They're rounding up human beings in Texas in a somehow more evil way than they normally do and I am contending with the three day refrigerated carcass of a $4.99 rotisserie chicken over the sink disgusting myself viscerally but still cleaning the bones in a way a natural predator would not bother to do. They would leave this detailing business to the scavenging birds and maggots. The payoff in calories not being worth the expense of the mouthing effort. No matter how many times I wash my hands after the grease will not come off.

It is autumn

A day or two after you had died they were already publishing stories about it in the newspaper. News of the Weird. A Rare Death. That kind of thing. Officials are calling it a Bizarre Incident.

You had set out on an October morning. Had kissed the sleeping missus on her forehead on the way out the door. Had settled into the brush and found your quiet and approached what you thought of as the all encompassing quiet of the world and after some waiting spotted a majestic 10-point whitetail buck drinking from the water.

You aimed.

Aimed.

Fired.

Knocked the son of a bitch clean over.

You were supposed to have waited longer before you went to inspect the kill man. To take your selfie. They're calling you a bozo online right now. You're getting cooked. The reverse of what you had planned. You filled the freezer.

Sudbury, Massachusetts

A baby was crying in the locker room. Its father had taken it to the pool to get out of the house and show it its first glimpses of the world I would reckon. I don't know what parents want. I do know what babies want though.

Now it was screaming mama mama. Over and over. Mama. Mama's not here right now the father said. I know that's a very common thing for a baby to cry out but there was something different about this. There was a dissonant harmony to it. Like a second voice speaking underneath its voice. Something akin to the bear in Annihilation. Like there was a fully formed human trapped and horrified at the body it found itself inside of.

The father was whispering to it and talking baby language like a parent does and it all knifed under my skin and peeled a layer off. This little baby's anguish.

I got dressed as quickly as I could to go walk out to my cold car in the cold slush of February and on the way I almost bumped into who I can only assume was Mama herself as there was a woman about the same age as the dad standing outside the locker room with a whole other forthcoming baby bulging out of her belly. It felt like seeing a famous writer on the street. I'm familiar with your work I wanted to say.

When I got into the car the sports talk radio station was playing loudly and they were talking about the Bruins and whether Brad Marchand deserved his suspension for beating a guy over the head with a stick and I started crying like I haven't in a long time. Sports talk radio on in the background while a middle aged guy cries in his car is probably not all that uncommon around here.

Mamaaaa ohhhooohhh.

I know it's not a big deal when a baby cries! I'm not fucking stupid. But I couldn't stop thinking about how it never asked for this. It never asked to be wrenched out of oblivion into this. To be dropped on a changing table at the shitty community pool where the scuba divers train and the dozens of children get yelled at for not swimming fast enough as I bob back and forth for twenty to thirty minutes a day depending on how hungover I am. For some reason the screaming at the beginning of life that we all do – the first thing any of us ever does is cry out for a mother we don't have the words for yet – made me think about men dying in trenches screaming for their own mothers and I wondered if any of all this was worth it.

It made me feel guilty too for never having given my wife a child that she wants so much.

Sometimes I don't know why a person would do that to a perfectly non-existent soul not existing right now nowhere. Bring it over here. The pool specifically but also everywhere I mean.

I said some of that to her later on that night. I was trying to explain how this baby's crying just completely tossed my entire world off its axis for a few hours and she said well would you rather have never been born and I thought about it for a minute and I said no because I would have never met you and she looked at me like alright pal settle down.

But that's silly I said because if I had never been anything I would never have done anything and I wouldn't know what I was missing one way or the other. Wouldn't that be the purest freedom?

Divine experience inherent in the everyday

If you ever catch me in a helicopter again it better be because they're saving my ass from a natural disaster. I had climbed inside of this one to do research for a travel magazine story and it was the stupidest thing I've ever done in my life.

The idea was that people could take a guided air tour of Paul Revere's ride and glide over the sites of some of the earliest battles of the Revolutionary War. Investigating history from altitude rather than depth like the rich dumbasses in the infamous submarine on the news all week.

I don't recall too many of the details of what I saw anymore because I was shitting my pants the entire time and half blacking out. Maybe it feels safer in a bigger helicopter but this Leonardo da Vinci bullshit could fit three people tops and not comfortably.

That's where you started shooting back at us the pilot laughed at one point. Nodding toward some historic field or other. He was a retired British soldier and I thought that seemed a little off. It would be like having Derek Jeter give you a tour of Fenway Park.

It's not so much that I'm scared of flying it's that I'm scared of only kind of flying I told the guy beforehand. I do ok on planes I said but it's the take off that frightens me. Being high up enough that you'd be absolutely fucked if anything went wrong but not yet high up enough that there would be time for the pilot to do something to forestall doom.

Speeding through the sky at hundreds of miles an hour is something most of us have done enough times now that it's sort of like whatever but just dinking around up there a thousand feet in the air is novel enough to feel unnatural.

I do not belong here I thought ten seconds into it.

A helicopter ride is a flight made up entirely of constant takeoffs.

Humans do not belong here.

I did my best to engage my writer brain in the midst of the panic attack. Jotting down observations in my notebook and smearing the ink with my sweaty palms. But by God the piece I was going to write! Poetry and history and the marvels of science. I was going to be the Henry Wadsworth Longfellow of the sky.

Well not even the sky. Just pretty high up.

Where does the sky actually begin?

"It's an informative, if a bit tense trip for those of us with a fear of heights," I wrote afterwards "but the distance of history, much like a bird's eye view of the landscape, has a way of changing one's perspective."

God being a writer is so dumb. The kind of shit you have to think of.

Not long after my editor said he only wanted like a hundred words for a front of the book blurb and cut everything out but the basic details of the tour package. I could've just as easily written it from land. I could've just copy and pasted the press release. I guess those submarine guys could have just looked at all the other videos we already have of the Titanic too.

Then I had to chase down the money they owed me for over a year.

I was relieved that it later turned out that the least worst bad thing happened to the people on board the submarine which is that they likely died instantly. I am certainly no fan of the ultra rich and wish many bad things upon them but even I draw the line at wanting them to be tortured and to die in such a slow agonizing horror.

Well maybe some of them should go that way but not as a blanket rule.

One of the most striking things about the wall to wall coverage of this fuck up I was interested in however was it happening just as a boat carrying 750 migrants sunk near Greece. Hundreds were missing and likely dead. I don't think I had even heard about it before the comparisons began and I basically live in the Clockwork Orange chair.

"It's a horrifying and disgusting contrast" someone from Human Rights watch said on the news. "The willingness to allow certain people to die while every effort is made to save others ... it's a really dark reflection on humanity," she said.

I don't think it was a nefarious plot by The Media to ignore the suffering of the poor although there is plenty of that baked into the traditional news gathering model. I think instead it's the decision makers seizing on an opportunity to give us something to be scared of that seems like it could happen to us. Sure very few of us could afford such a specific excursion but we could certainly go on another kind of trip and find ourselves imperiled. Mountain climbing or skiing or scuba diving or some such. We could all imagine ourselves trapped somewhere and running out of air or food or water and panicking and facing the grim knowledge that you are likely to die.

But why can so many people picture themselves in a situation like that or something like it on one kind of boat but not on another? Not on one packed with hundreds of people dying in the water in a slightly different way? Something that people all over the world do regularly. Are doing right now.

We're all a lot closer to becoming like those poor migrants lost at sea than we are to being roguish billionaire explorers. It may not feel like it from the relevant comfort of our lives such as they are right now but it's the truth. It would probably take some work but I'm confident I could get there with a sustained series of really bad choices and some moderately bad luck.

On the other hand there are no choices I could possibly make now or ever that would elevate me to the level of the fabulously wealthy.

Most of us reading this right now are merely hovering in the low sky. We can see the land right there down below us. We're probably not going to crash. This thing isn't going to crash right? It's safe right?

Another house

There's me on the roof lounge of an expensive hotel by the water revising the longest and most interminable suicide note anyone had ever heard of. A train was hooting by and a barge was groaning by and a canoodling couple a few couches down were waking up from their invisibility. Returning from the pocket universe where no single other human is real nor has ever been real besides the one whose body you are holding. And here to greet them was the sight of yours truly crushing out a cigarette I had burned down to the smelly chemical part of the filter then hucking a half-full champagne glass toward the muddy river. Not even coming close to reaching it. Like a Hail Mary that gets batted down at the 10 yard line. Everyone booing my bullshit. Get him the fuck out of there.

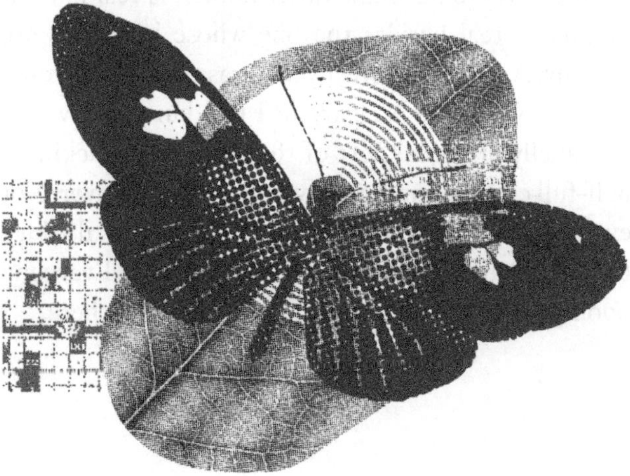

**All of us were here for a little while
and then we were somewhere else**

I started watching the Game Show Network right around when the pandemic and middle age and suburbia all hit me concurrently none of which I have yet to and will likely never rebound from and something I still can't get over years later watching anew every evening eating our little coffee table dinner is how on most of the games every contestant is this kind of pure grotesquerie from California which is the most uncanny state in America the most uncanny country in creation. I'm reminded of when I used to watch Nathan For You and I'd think it's a trick it's all actors but no it's just that people there are like that. Californians are a species who simply want to be able to drive two miles in under 90 minutes if they're lucky and who love to be insane. No one will ever figure them out. Not Steinbeck or Hammett or Lynch or Chandler or Didion or West or Tarantino.

Ahhh shit a millipede or something like that an associate of the overarching millipede enterprise just skittered past me and I made a noise that I'm not exactly proud of. It was a pretty big one too.

It's pouring rain in Massachusetts today and cold already this early in September and I've seen some of these types of guys in the basement before so this had better not be the harbinger of an exodus of some kind.

I flailed for something to kill it with out of instinct and it was quicker than I was and ran for cover and now it's gone to the limbo where nightmares have their smoke break.

The spiders have been finding their way inside too now that it's getting colder. I just saw a remarkable one outside this morning while taking out the trash. It had erected one of the most elaborate webs I've ever seen. Adjusting for scale it was like a spider mansion. One with craftsmanship behind it. Holding up in the downpour better than even the spider itself probably would have ever dreamed. You could imagine the other older spiders coming over to admire it and they'd all be standing around going now that's a proper web until whoever the biggest one was decided to eat everybody.

I was trying so hard earlier to think of the other California writer I wanted to mention above in my little list there and all I could recall was that I had posted a picture of the book that I can't remember on Instagram roughly ten years ago which isn't an especially efficient mechanism for remembering books. I scrolled down and down and down into my past aging myself in reverse and there it was in 2012 sitting on the side table of a California hotel.

Ask the Dust by John Fante.

Let me look up a couple of quotes from it real quick to jog my memory.

"All of us were here for a little while, and then we were somewhere else; we were not alive at all; we approached living, but we never achieved it. We are going to die. Everybody was going to die."

"I looked at the faces around me and I knew mine was like theirs. Faces with the blood drained away, tight faces, worried, lost. Faces like flowers torn from their roots and stuffed into a pretty vase, the colors draining fast. I had to get away from that town."

Yeah that definitely sounds like the type of shit that I would have liked back then. Now too but especially back then.

I have only been to California five or seven or ten times and I don't really know what I'm talking about. About California specifically but also anything.

There was the time I was young and definitely going to be a rock star making a record there and the time a girl took me home and the house was peculiar looking and not knowing anything about architecture I didn't realize until much later she was a descendant of the main California architecture guy and the time I was almost going to work at Instagram haha and did all these interviews at the fake town they have there and the time I've talked about before bumming out Elliott Smith at the Troubadour and the time with John Legend and a hot air balloon and the time on the beach by the iconic rock formations where another girl started to sour on me and the times in

San Francisco getting mugged every five minutes due to woke prosecutors.

One night my friend took me to an indoor hotel pool tiki bar way up on a hill and then I spent the rest of the trip trying to drink in as many famous cocktail spots as possible and shortening my life drink by drink.

How many more drinks will it be before it all turns?

It was the fourth of July and it was so cold. We stood on a roof watching the muted fireworks through a mile of fog thinking this fucking sucks. No one told me to bring a winter coat to the fourth of July in northern California.

Mark Twain did I suppose.

Sometimes people from over there try to tell me that the water is just as if not colder than it is here in New England and while I logically accept that they are probably right I still do not believe it. How your brain won't let itself process things you don't want to believe.

Another girl I once loved is standing by that very same cold Californian water and looking prettier than the ocean. She's adjusting how she's posing and trying out different looks while I'm getting ready to take the picture. I'm going hold on hold on ok here we go wait hold on and then she smiles and goes come on is it a video and I go haha got you again. We had a good laugh about that classic gag even though we were pretty miserable at the time if I'm being honest. Were probably not going to make it out of that one.

And did not.

Most things I try to remember about having been in California feel like they happened on some sitcom I watch to fall asleep to. Not because many of them are filmed there but more so that I usually don't remember the plot or the dialogue of my own experiences and it's all operating there in my subconscious in the background fucking me up from the past even when I'm not paying attention.

Don't misunderstand me I love it there and I want to be there right now although I just saw it's 110 degrees today so maybe scrap this whole idea.

Also there are the fires and the droughts to consider.

Nonetheless I am pulled there in a type of longing specific to me but also with the same cliche longing we all have in common for the West. That has called people there forever with all the songs and movies and all of it. How if the continent were a table and you turned it on its side and gravity came into play we would all tumbled westward. I'm pulled both by the idea of freedom and the expanse the land itself represents in the American mythology but also the lie of the myth. I want to experience the lie. The make believe of it all that people know is make believe but let themselves operate inside of anyway.

Being lied to isn't so bad sometimes compared to being aware of how things actually are. You wouldn't want to go around like that for very long. No one wants to know all the secrets.

By the way I know it sucks to live in California in the same way it sucks to live anywhere in America and in a lot of ways more so than anywhere else but the heart wants what it wants.

The girl I love now and I talk about taking a trip somewhere but the thing is I don't want to take a trip anywhere I want to actually be somewhere else. I want to live somewhere else besides an hour from where I was born and guess what I never will. It's just this for the rest of my run.

Maybe when we're older we say sometimes. Maybe we'll go somewhere when we're old.

Donald Trump is on the TV. He's an evil disgusting piece of shit and maybe our worst living human being who I hope has ____ by the time this comes out but every now and again he says something accidentally poignant.

"And remember, Florida's easier than other places. You have the ocean and you have the sun. There's something about that that works."

He was speaking in Las Vegas.

"But, you have the sun, too, but you don't have the ocean. I can tell. You definitely don't have the ocean. Maybe someday you'll have the ocean, you never know."

"Someday. Hopefully it's a long time away, right? Hopefully."

> *"Maybe someday you'll have the ocean."*
> *Ahead was a mounted policeman in khaki directing traffic. He raised his baton. The car slowed suddenly pressing him against me.*
> *"Yes," I said. "Isn't it pretty to think so?"*

Could be I'm just reading pathos into it because it also sounds like something a girl might say after she leaves me.

Whatever girl. Every girl I ever knew.

"Maybe someday you'll have the ocean."

That is honestly all I do want. I have never really cared much about money or becoming wealthy or famous or anything like that I just want to someday to live by the ocean. To have the ocean.

I wonder about this impulse I have to drink and to smoke all the time two things that undeniably will make me die sooner than I would have otherwise and you would think there is some death drive thing going on there some desire for nothingness but it's the opposite of that for me. I am terrified of dying almost every hour of the day I am awake and a few of them when I am asleep.

Something changed about the way I dream in the past few months. My dreams used to be disjointed and abstract and absurd jumbles of unconnected vignettes that dissolved if you tried to catch them upon waking but now they're consistent scenes with a coherent plot and identifiable people familiar to me who behave like normal people behave albeit with the tension heightened significantly. And when I wake up I can remember them and they follow me around for a lot longer than they used to. Maybe it's something metaphysical or maybe it's just that I take more vitamins now before going to bed and they fuck with my brain water.

I'm not sure if either of those types of dreaming are common for most people or not. I have no idea what other people's dreams are like and could be that's exactly the problem for all of us. I guess we all dream about going to California and "going to California" but despite all of the books and movies made about the literal act of that and the metaphorical act of that none of us have ever been able to agree about what going to California means.

The game shows though. There's this one called America Says hosted by John Michael Higgins who is an absolute pro and a delight (and from Boston by the way). You will know him from the Christopher Guest movies and more recently from everyone being mad that his character in Licorice Pizza was racist. I don't particularly have a take on that movie besides that it was some real California shit.

America Says is kind of like Family Feud in which teams called THE DOG PEOPLE or CHURCH PALS or THE UNEMPLOYED LA ACTORS TRYING

TO GET ON TAPE have to answer questions based on surveys. Family Feud has more money so they can fly contestants in from around the country to showcase how uncanny America is on the macro level but the other shows like this just have to recruit people at the Glendale Galleria or whatever so it's mostly the Californians.

In the final round the teams often get caught up on one of the clues like they were so close to winning the fifteen grand but they just could not clean the board and there's this moment when the mean sounding buzzer goes off and they all stand there frowning and feeling dumb doing the aw shucks motions like you'd expect someone who just lost to do but more than that more than anything else they're waiting for our man to turn over the missed answers so they can understand just how it was that they lost.

So they're standing there dejected on TV thinking that if they learn the mistake that they had just made it will make it easier to accept the losing after the fact. Needing to comprehend what went wrong despite not being able to go back and change anything either way.

It's like when you hear about someone dying that you only kind of know or used to know and you want to be able grasp how their passing transpired which has happened to me more times than I care to reflect on right now in the past few years like to my old musician friend in California a couple months ago for example. People you know enough to mourn but not enough to be officially looped in on the specifics. HOW DID HE DIE WHAT WAS IT? you want to scream at everyone but you can't always ask that. You can't walk into the room they died inside of like a doctor and look at the chart and frown.

The impulse is to want to understand whether or not you have to worry about losing in the same way as these poor assholes did or if you would have known the correct answer to counteract the riddle. If you would have survived long enough to show up on the next episode.

And how did that make you feel?

I was telling this woman every bad thing I had ever done in my life but she didn't seem particularly impressed. She had a look like the toll booth lady when you'd hand her money out of the car window on the Mass Pike back when you still had to do that.

I had finally managed to find a new therapist on the computer after a couple dozen said I wasn't their problem or my insurance company told me to go fuck myself so I was sitting there with the sunny window behind me making me look like shit on the Zoom. It seemed like she was distracted and probably had her own thing going on in fairness. At one point she was bouncing a kid she pulled from offstage out of nowhere onto her lap and that's... fine (?) How expensive childcare is now.

So I was off my game and out of practice for how to talk in therapy or talk to anyone. Normally you sort of flirt with a new therapist early on so they'll like you and want to fix your brain more than if you are just some guy who more evidently sucks.

The thing was her Boston accent was just way too much. Even for me sounding how I sound. It ruined my ability to suspend my disbelief. It was the inverse of when you watch a movie and the fake accents they're doing are so bad it throws you off. Instead the accent was too authentic. It caused this whole metaphysical collapse in my mind about what is real or not. I thought is this lady fucking with me?

There's something comforting about hearing the voice you grew up with reflected back to you in a way that engenders instinctual trust and fellowship. Like if you meet a guy from Somerville in London or wherever. Go Celtics haha. All that. But sometimes it's the exact same voice that belongs to everyone who was ever cruel to you when you were young. The very reason you were going to therapy in the first place.

iii.

There was a fresh sinkhole in the middle of town that had done considerable damage and so we all went down to gawk. Me and Allan standing close but not that close based on prior misadventure. Inspecting it passive aggressively like Italian grandfathers outside of a construction site. Sizing up the workmanship of God or whoever dug it. Thinking we could have done a better job if only given the chance. If only given back our old tools. The padlocked chains on the shed door having long since rusted shut. There was another one a few towns over that people were saying was so big that you could see it from space but what did that perspective do for anyone down here? Who could possibly be looking that could help?

You can only have them when they're dead

There are police helicopters hovering over the hotel you are staying in.

Now they are gone.

Shit now one is coming back around again.

Somebody must have fucked up.

Maybe someone running for their life.

You do not sleep well in hotels anymore. The state of these pillows now. Made for studier necks.

Your snoring wife was over-served maple old fashioneds at her new friend's backyard fire pit in the near suburbs of Portland while the husband showed you his workman shed. It was very nicely built in all sincerity. You asked about the electrical wiring. I understand that's the part you don't want to fuck up you said.

No you definitely do not he said.

He was going to put in a skylight next.

They had visited his parents in Pensacola recently and watched a famous jet squadron perform synchronized stunts from a boat amidst a sea of political flags.

My father and I don't talk about it he said. It's the only way he said and you said you understood.

You just let go of it he said.

Later at the hotel lobby bar they were playing an MF Doom playlist and the broccolini in duck fat scrapings that you ordered was $23.

All the servers seemed suspiciously skinny and suspiciously Slavic and there's nothing wrong with either of those things it's just how they seemed to you.

Man I love this song you told the bartender when Souls of Mischief came on and he said they make us listen to this.

Smoke from the snow-wettened wood fire was blowing directly into your face and after some silence your wife said you both had gone to the Louisa May Alcott Orchard House the other day. Trading stories of places you had been recently like couples on couples dates do.

It's where she wrote Little Women she said.

Oh my god I loved that movie the wife said.

The thing is the ceilings were so low you said. The whole time I was standing there I was thinking about how I could reach up and punch my fists through them if I wanted to.

No one knows what to say to anyone anymore.

Why would you think something like that your wife said.

Well I didn't actually want to do it.

The ceilings were very low though she agreed.

How little were these women you said.

The guy fake laughed but he made you wait a beat for it.

There was a pretty big storm while they were down in Florida the wife said.

So we're miles inland the guy said taking over now. Commandeering the ship. And we wake up at my parents house and I go outside and there are fish all over the place in the yard. On the sidewalk. The weird part was they weren't dying. They were inching around like they could walk. Not even that slowly really. Pushing themselves forward with their fins.

What kind of fish were they you asked and she tagged back in and said apparently they're called walking catfish.

Name checks out you said.

All of these little mucus gray fish marching around the driveway he said.

Do you think it meant anything your wife asked her.

Like how do you mean?

I don't know. Biblically I guess.

Well I don't know either she said. Nothing good she said.

There are weird laws about invasive species down there the guy said. Legally speaking you can only have them when they're dead he said. Possess them when they're dead. So my mom came out and swept a bunch of them out into the street off the property line and the ones that didn't get the hint my dad came out and stuck them with a spear.

Tell them about the bald eagle your wife said.

Ah well it's not much of a story you said but it's kind of funny.

They found an eagle in the park the next town over from ours. But it wasn't really moving around much. Not flying anywhere. A pretty clear sign of something being wrong. Just sitting there in the grass by a soccer game. Like it was a bored parent. Everyone was taking selfies with it and trying to get as close as they could without it lashing out. Some of the kids got worried that it was injured. It became kind of a local celebrity for a couple days.

So they called the bird people over. Whoever handles the birds. They called those guys. And they brought it in and checked it out and gave it an X-ray and everything and when they looked inside of it they found two entire racoon paws digesting there in its distended stomach.

They said the thing wasn't injured it was just too fat to fly.

I know how that is haha the guy said patting his belly and you laughed but you made him wait a beat for it.

He didn't even have a big belly so it felt like stolen valor.

The hotel door guy kept opening the door for you every time you went outside to smoke in the cold which in fairness was a major part of his job description. You wanted to ask him to stop doing it. To tell him that this isn't necessary. None of this is. You greased his palm hoping he would look the other way next time but that just made him want to open the door for you even more.

Maybe people aren't supposed to get hotel bar drunk in a hotel bar the way you used to be able to. A person could get a good way toward killing themselves like that before any of these people were born. Everyone is so much younger than that now.

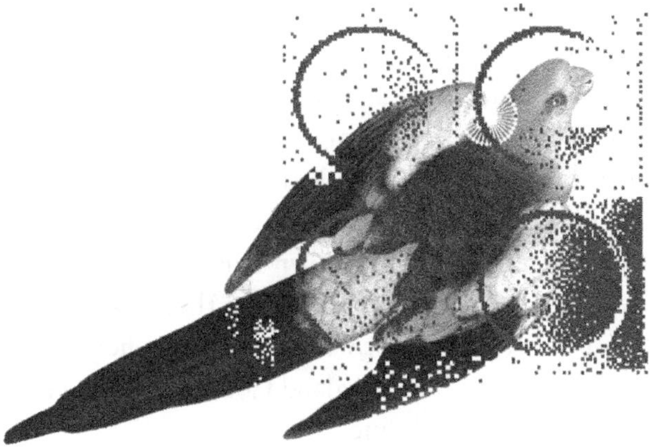

Dead mall rodeo

Eight bulls escaped from a rodeo at the Emerald Square Mall In North Attleboro on Sunday. Big honking ones too. They hauled ass right through a fence like it was nothing my buddy said. Then they stampeded off across the parking lot before people lost track of them in the woods behind the Dunkies.

It wasn't long before the fire department went racing after them but it was unclear to me what expertise they had in this kind of predicament. Inside of the animals was a type of fire that water cannot extinguish. I was going to say they should have sent in a team of cowboys but look how that worked out to begin with. Maybe they'd have to fly in some of the more talented ones from down south. A bull negotiator of some kind if that is a thing that they have.

I didn't even know we had rodeos up here I said.

You can be New England Country now my buddy said and I said yeah fine.

Did you hear that one singer or one of those guys bought a house down on Duxbury beach he said and I said wow that's crazy. The kind of shit you say about something that is very normal.

Later on the news they had a bunch of locals on talking about how scary the event was and how lucky they were that they hadn't been gored to death. One lady said they came this close to trampling her into the bushes.

I was mostly surprised that the cops hadn't slaughtered them all on the spot.

Eventually seven of the bulls found their way into some guy's backyard. The eighth was still at large presumably. The guy was laughing about it now that the excitement had mostly died down. He said he had hustled his dogs inside and he and his kids went up on the roof. Like they did before and later to take refuge from the flood. They watched the bulls run around in a circle for a while until it got too cold out and he had to get the kids to go to bed.

It was an almost hypnotizing kind of pattern he said. How they were circling. The boys had gotten their nerf guns out for protection. It was like getting a free rodeo the guy said. No he'd never even been to one before he said.

One of the bulls started playing with a soccer ball for a while. Nosing it back and forth from one side of the yard to the other. Chasing after it when it rolled off. The rest never stopped their pacing to join in. Never even looked over at the other one. Maybe it still thought it was on the clock and felt like it had to put on a show. Or did it sense for the first time ever that it briefly did not.

Which side are you on?

We drove into Cambridge and got on the T at Alewife the last stop on the Red Line heading inbound and I felt depressed about having to do that. Having to commute to a protest.

I get anxious before any protest. In large part because of the ever present threat of things going sideways via police-instigated violence. That's not the anxiety I mean in this case though.

The thing I'm talking about is that I was worried no one else was going to come. Like it was a party I was hosting or a show I was playing.

I had nothing to do with this protest to be clear. Besides the ways we are all a part of every protest either actively or in absentia.

I didn't have to worry about anyone coming for very long though. The T was packed. More than usual. It was slow walking up the Park Street stairs. They said around 30,000 people showed up between speeches on the Boston Common and a march to City Hall Plaza for the main event. Some reported 100,000. I don't know about that number but you could believe it for a minute standing there in the massive crowd.

One of the weird things about being in a protest march is that you usually have no concept of how big it is while it is happening. You have to find out about that later. In the meantime you can only see the bodies around you.

That is also one of the best and most important aspects of attending a protest. Seeing and feeling the bodies around you. Feeling part of something larger than yourself.

"The importance of the numbers involved is to be found in the direct experience of those taking part in or sympathetically witnessing the demonstration," as John Berger wrote. "For them the numbers cease to be numbers and become the evidence of their senses, the conclusions of their imagination."

No one on my feeds the past 48 hours will shut the fuck up about the right way to protest. The group behind the protests this weekend around the country that millions of people came out for may or may not be the same old Democrat bullshit. I do not know and I don't really give a shit right now. I will tell you what is true and that is that tens of thousands of us marched and chanted and listened for hours as speakers from all manner of political groups I am excited about and ones I am skeptical of came together for one thing we can agree upon which is that this country – this evil fucking country that we all despise and yet must continue to live in for better or worse – is being dismantled and sold off for parts for the benefit of Donald Trump and Elon Musk and their rich friends.

If you object to this ravaging then you and I have a place to begin negotiating from.

M. and I stood in the cold 40 degree rain and cheered and booed. Everyone fucking hates Elon

Musk this much is clear. People hate this guy's fucking guts. That is raw material to work with. A person like him should not exist. No billionaire should. It is not that many steps from one idea to the other. You can guide a person there no matter their politics.

I don't think I saw more than one or two cops which was kind of unsettling in the moment and also in retrospect. Some said it was because this march was largely white people but I don't know how they would have known to know that beforehand.

Ah shit I just remembered the existence of the pervasive surveillance state.

I do not know about elsewhere but it was largely younger people of color on stage for us in Boston despite the crowd being mostly older white people or else younger parents with their sign-waving kids. God there were so many corny signs. Ed Markey and Ayanna Pressley and Michelle Wu all spoke and were mostly fine. Occasionally inspiring. There was also a lot of talk about protecting immigrants and labor and students – Rümeysa Öztürk in particular – and trans people and native people and yes even a bunch of mentions of Gaza from the stage and a lot from the crowd. Hands off Gaza was chanted at this rally.

I almost teared up a couple times man.

I'm sorry but for all their faults I still love Boston and Massachusetts so much.

America on the other hand.

I told M. I was libbing out a little bit. Everyone's a little bit of a lib at a protest like this we joked and then we looked over at the people near us waving Palestinian flags and banging a drum and screaming like hell at Markey and Pressley and thought hmm maybe not everyone.

Good I thought.

Get them.

I've talked a lot lately about the buoying effect of simply getting out there. Getting off your ass. Off the computer. I had forgotten for a while but it is indeed true. It is different.

My back didn't even hurt standing there the whole time. What a miracle. I was being held up.

I bumped into Ken out of the Dropkicks and took a selfie like a dork. He acted like he remembered me and that was nice of him. His band played Which Side Are You On? at the end of the day as the rain really started to fall and that was the only thing I thought about on the way home and for the rest of the weekend. It's an old question and one labor movements are intimately familiar with but I hope all the other people who were there and maybe never really asked it of themselves are doing so now.

I hope the people at home who didn't come out this time might start to feel the weight of that question tugging at their consciences.

Ok great that all sounds like a nice little day so now what? That's a good question but I didn't see the need to ask it in the middle of one concrete example of what out of many. While a possible first step was happening.

Protesting isn't the only thing but it is one of the things.

Now what is the same problem we had a couple of days and weeks and months and years ago. But I bet a lot of people this weekend found neighbors they can try to figure it out with together.

"Those who take part become more positively aware of how they belong to a class," to quote Berger again. "Belonging to that class ceases to imply a common fate, and implies a common opportunity."

Listen to me I still hate these donation-seekers who tell us a better future is only possible by chipping in $10 to their organizations. But if this isn't an example of millions of people around the country ripe to be organized and ushered into a new understanding that a better world than this is possible then I don't know what is.

All protests are different in their own way but at the heart of them they are all usually pretty simple:

It doesn't have to be this way.

I refuse to let it be this way.

We refuse to let it be this way.

Where the Old Mouth used to be

I was trying to get this toddler to like me. Mostly because no one else here seemed to thus far. A last ditch attempt at meaningful human connection. Besides it was a much lower barrier for entry. How children are stupid.

All of which amounted to kicking a rapidly deflating beach ball back and forth. Honestly the kid fucking sucked at kicking the ball but you can't berate them for being bad at sports because that is their father's job so you just gotta go good kick buddy and then do the half ass jog across the yard to retrieve the ball they shanked into the brush. You can't talk to them anymore like my father talked to me and his father talked to him stretching back as far as the history of fathers and kicking balls has been recorded. Just kick the ball right you want to say. Just stop being an alcoholic they want to say in return.

At a lovely beach house on the south shore of Massachusetts. Near where my lawyer lives actually. With in-laws of in-laws piling on top of one another which is a largely unremarked upon dynamic of the extended family tree. What is the husband of your sister in-law's sister in-law to you besides Some Guy?

It always feels to me like when they first introduced interleague play. These people should not be on the field together. Or when they used to have them all wear their distinctive uniforms on the field for the all-star game.

Which was cool actually so never mind that's a bad analogy.

No wait now that I think of it that guy is not just Some Guy. Some Guy is simple and easy. Some Guy has no frame of reference. How when you're at a barbecue or a wedding as a better example and you're standing there and Some Guy is standing there too and you go well I better talk to this asshole or else it's weird and you go oh hey man how do you know the couple and he goes I don't actually I just got called up from the minors. This is my first at bat. I'm trying to fuck some lady a lot more so here I am at this.

Not that but essentially.

You go uh so what do you do man? Hoping he won't ask the same of you.

Meanwhile at the beach house there was a squirrel posted up on a large tree clinging upside down and barking and barking. Staring daggers at something in the near distance. Do squirrels usually bark? This one doing it anyway without looking like its mouth was even moving. Like the bark was issuing from out of the center of its body. Squirrel bark not tree bark. The tail thumping and sort of poorly keeping time like an addict drummer. I have seen so many squirrels and so many addict drummers for that matter but I have never heard one of them make a sound like this. Like a cat trying to speak dog. Growling and hissing atonally.

This squirrel would not break eye contact with one specific point not very far away and he was carrying on so much I thought there must be a larger than normal snake or a coyote or what have you just over there in the dunes and I finally got up and walked over to inspect the situation with a fearlessness that was short lived and then got a little nervous in a way that embarrassed me. What if it really were a monster of some kind stalking us for his supper and this squirrel was doing us a service the entire time? A Lassie type of deal.

Then the kid kicked the ball at my head and I was like haha wow good one buddy and the door to the house opened and out spilled an entire column of children squealing like the Kill Bill siren with no earthly idea that there might be a bear or a rabid dog or whatever you please in the vicinity.

Now I was outnumbered by them.

I had this thought out of nowhere that when I grow sick I want you and our kids and the doctor and everyone to lie to me about what's actually happening. To tell me I have way more time than I actually do. All the time in the world in fact. To tell me the results came in and the lab guy said it was basically no big deal at all and that I am free to go.

And then when it's your turn I'll do likewise.

To feel like a wrongly incarcerated man released and breathing in fresh air for the first time in a decade.

The newspaper coming down to take a photo.

Nobody wants to see it coming. Sensing it circling you and barking out helplessly from a place you thought was safe.

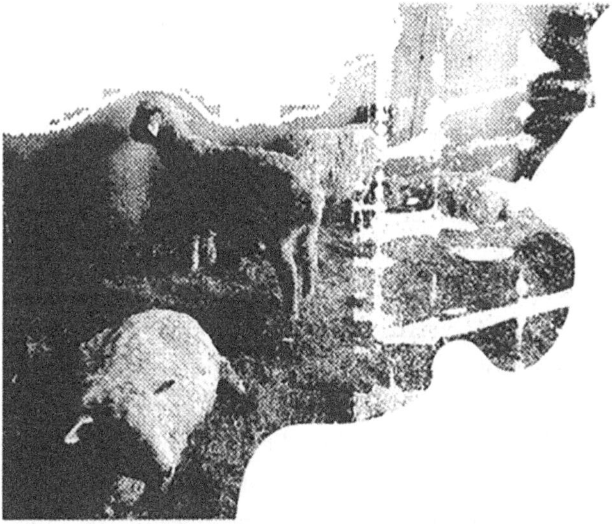

Like a condemned man

I had this disgusting shudder just now of my disgusting youth where my disgusting bandmates and I would stay up all night and sometimes all night again struggling to make one another grasp how important this or that The Smiths or The Cure song was and after every other topic was exhausted it would typically come to a point where we would start debating which substance it was worse to run out of as we were inevitably running out of all of them.

Like astronauts on a derelict spaceship watching the oxygen levels decline. Checking the mess for food. The water purifier still functioning.

Maybe a meteor storm coming that the radar didn't pick up. All of us dead yet and not knowing it.

Was it cigarettes or coke or alcohol?

Each of us rendered a different judgment.

Sure no one ever wanted an unlimited supply of coke in the bargaining. Perhaps just a little taste more for now if you can spare it haha and maybe one more for the road obviously and one for the pillow but unlimited would be a nightmare let's be serious. Enough alcohol to drink yourself off to the other dimension when all is said and done yes that is crucial. Load bearing. But a cigarette as punctuation is the chief thing. Drinking and using coke are not worth it without the final cigarette as best as I could tell them. Tell you.

Like a condemned man about to be executed needs a cigarette.

Now that I think of it maybe it's the cigarette that needs the condemned man to realize its significance? Not even the overtly condemned criminal man just the standard condemned man which is all of us.

When you're an addict you get to relive the feeling of being executed every night before bed. Usually it doesn't take and you fall through the trap door and come out the other side like holy shit I'm alive what the fuck. But sooner or later the device generally works as it is intended to.

It will be withheld

You went to a funeral yesterday for a man you did not know very well but who was nonetheless a lovely and interesting man as far as you could tell. Was beloved by dozens which is pretty good. Not so bad in the accounting of it all.

They read Tennyson's Crossing the Bar at his service.

You hadn't been to mass in a good while but almost everything was familiar to you still. Almost every word of every prayer and almost every song and every movement up and down and up and down and you cried a little despite not having a close connection to this old man because one thing you will always do is you will cry at every funeral that you ever go to.

Every wedding too.

Every single thing that ever happens to anyone either good or bad.

It's all too much.

After the service you all drove behind each other slowly and badly to a restaurant on the water and ate shitty lemony fish and warm creamy pasta out of steam trays. Too early to drink you thought at first but then everyone else was getting after it so then what did it matter if you joined them.

After a few you walked outside and down the street and up onto the stout seawall and invented a guy to get mad at. Someone you haven't met yet who later ends up crying at your funeral some number of years from now.

Negotiating the amount of years with yourself to not seem like a liar to yourself.

What will this guy mean to me you thought. Or to whoever some guy is to anyone?

Or to whoever you are to anyone.

The surf was kind of phoning it you noticed. You had been expecting swells after the recent storm.

You stared out at the expanse of the world hoping to have some kind of epiphany.

It doesn't work like that though. When you're forcing it. You have to have let your guard down for the ocean to sneak up on you.

It's like when a cat knows you want affection. Or a cruel partner.

They will withhold it.

It will be withheld.

You pictured your fictional future bereaved standing on this very block just over there by the fireworks store. A belly full of fish. Another fucking liar.

The voices of children can be heard from under the rubble

Everyone was in agreement that they did not believe in Hell anymore per se. Was it even mentioned in the Bible after all? But also that they nevertheless wished that it were in fact real. If only for the sake of these goddamned bastards.

For a limited time being of course. Nothing eternal. Nothing drastic like that. We weren't monsters ourselves.

And I do too. I also wish that. I stood up and told them that. Hat in hand. Even teared up a little bit. It was a rousing speech someone said afterwards looking me directly in the eye and shaking my hand like a senator. Telling me there were people he wanted me to come and meet out back.

But we have to be careful about what we collectively dream into being I said. I am pretty sure that this is how they invented it the first time around.

By the intensity with which something is being said

One of the bad storms was on the TV. It was one of the ones that was bad enough that the guys down at the TV station thought that they could make good money off of it by showing it on a loop all night. The apartment buildings genuflecting into the surf and the wind shaving the trees bald and the rest of it. And so I sat there watching for hours on a Tuesday only partly on account of there was no basketball on. Meanwhile my eyes were darting toward the window every time a branch outside of my own questionably built home groaned in the local and altogether unrelated wind.

Unless all wind is related then never mind.

It was pointless for me to worry about because the famous TV storm was a thousand miles away and storms aren't that big just yet that they can touch all of us at the same time. I kept doing it anyway like everything else I knew was stupid and kept doing.

The sound of my trees bowing outside was like when you've woken from a nightmare and the whining floorboards are transposed into an intruder's footfalls.

Of late I've been having the one again where I'm a waiter in the weeds getting sat with five tables at once then ten then fifteen one after the next and I am trying so hard but I simply cannot manage to greet each of them and the layout of the Escheresque restaurant mutates into foolishness. I can't even water them to buy time and what's worse it's my first day but also I'm returning after a long absence and I don't know the menu yet or anymore and then I burst out of that and gasp and now there's a psychopath smiling at the foot of the bed who looks like they can see the future in short increments and then I burst out of that and it's just all of all of this.

Not entirely sure which scenario I'd prefer at this point in my life the tables or the killer or reality.

On the TV the asphalt shingled roof of a treacly cocktail blue home was being cracked in half like a chest cavity on a billion year old heart surgeon's table.

I thought of sitting at the foot of my grandfather's ottoman on a vulgar musty carpet as he watched the kind of storms we used to have on the kind of TVs we used to have and how the kind of reporters we used to have presented it all in a jargon I didn't speak and still don't in terms of wave surges and specific categories of wind power but much like when you're unequipped to translate a foreign language you can nonetheless glean the necessary information by the intensity with which something is being said. The same way as when you're a kid and dumb you basically get what is transpiring with the adults in the room on the other side of your wall when the yelling is going on. Or maybe when you're traveling and someone is furious or laughing or scared out of their mind and it breaks through your denseness no matter what language they're suffering inside of.

A person begging for their life communicates in a universal tongue.

I watched just now how this one reporter's jacket rippled like a blown flag in the gale much like it always would have but some degree more dangerously today. A newer more intense jacket for a newer more intense wind.

Haha you better get out of that storm soon the anchor in the TV studio always used to go and was still going now. The same patter.

Haha I will the other guy would go and was still going now. The atmospheric pressure is… getting real…uh big he'd go or whatever it was he used to say and is saying now.

Listen they should've emphasized this nautical catastrophe shit a lot more when I was young. I don't know what to tell you.

I could tell you about some Emily Dickinson or Raymond Carver poems perhaps. I'm not going to but I could.

A friend posted the other day asking whether or not Emily Dickinson had a Boston accent which I don't think checks out but I'm going to pretend she did because it's funnier that way.

> *And with ironic caw*
> *Flap past it to the*
> *Farmer's corn*
> *Men eat of it and die*

More importantly all the while there's this reporter and his news crew by the van guzzling down barrels of sea spray and trying to maintain composure like when you're drunker than you want to let on to people who don't love you. So it's easier for them to look the other way. The guy clenching every muscle in his body and desperately bracing himself on a street pole just a second or two more than he might have wanted to and traveling into the realm where a brave man momentarily becomes a coward. A shuddering premonition of blackness in the shuddering wind of a storm.

I just looked away from the storm and toward my phone and read something that a famous horror writer I like said about being in the hospital.

"I've had surgery a number of times, and coming back into consciousness subsequent to anesthesia has made me realize just how great it is to lie in a black oblivion. I genuinely hope I die on an operating table."

Buddy no. That's the opposite of what we're supposed to want. Even accounting for how a horror type of guy has to present himself in public.

It's the return from the black oblivion that is the euphoria right? I feel like that's obvious. The first thing you can taste after the dentist when your jaw had been numbed. After a while you relearn what a potato chip is supposed to crunch like. When a cold passes and you know again how beautiful it is to be able to smell the world even if what you're smelling is shit.

I went for a run the other day back on Cape Cod back where my grandfather watched TV and I followed a path I was unfamiliar with along the tall reeds down by the unblown still river and stumbled across some horses standing there in their little horse congregating area and the smell knocked me back into fifty different episodes of my life.

Can you imagine if our sense of smell was as powerful as it is for dogs and other animals while our human brains stayed as complicated as they are? Just constantly being hammered with memories of every moment we've ever lived all at once every day forever. We'd be cutting our noses off. Like a man driven insane by the recollection of untold horrors gouges out his eyes for relief from the maddening sensory onslaught.

I don't want any of that blackness shit to be clear. I don't want to die suddenly I want to die slowly. So slowly that you can see death coming for many thousands of miles incrementally on an alien horizon. Like a sudden foreign moon cresting. From a very young age until a very old age and it just keeps getting closer and closer but never quite reaches you until it does and it's undeniable.

Not much I can do here you'd say.

To finally not have any poor choices left to make is a kind of liberation.

How a cigarette tastes for a person dying of cancer. When they don't have to have that possibility hanging over them anymore. They're off the hook.

Have you ever had a friend who is dying from something else more blameless and he knows it's coming and you know it's coming but you still want to make him laugh one more time for the road every time you see him for what might be the last time? Are you sure you can't hang out a while longer bud you go and he goes ah I better be going. You give one last try at it but don't want to show that you're thinking about what is happening here as a kindness and he knows that that is what you're doing.

Maybe it's like when you know it's the last time you're going to fuck someone you love and they know it too but you both still try hard for some reason with the fucking. A retiring athlete's last game but the fanbase is one single other person and it will all collapse imminently with the entire franchise disbanded and erased from the record books.

That's all a part of another stupid series of things I think.

Lots of people are sharing a passage from William Shatner's book this week. In it he recounts his trip to the edge of space with one of the richest men to ever live. The mysteries of the universe and the hypotheses about how all of this came to be have thrilled him his entire life he wrote but as they left Earth he looked out toward the infinite expanse and thought "there was no mystery, no majestic awe to behold . . . all I saw was death."

"I saw a cold, dark, black emptiness. It was unlike any blackness you can see or feel on Earth...My trip to space was supposed to be a celebration; instead, it felt like a funeral."

I looked at a painting after reading that.

> *Damned souls protest in vain and try to deny the colossal and minutely detailed account of sins, foolishnesses and assorted wicked things that they committed in life. Detail from the Triptyque de l'Apocalypse by Jacobello Alberegno ca. 1390.*

Elsewhere some guys on my phone were arguing over whether or not they could win a fight against a goose and I believe I could do it although I know that's stupid too.

Just grab its neck one of them said.

Just easily grab the furious goose's neck.

Swinging it around like Big Papi hitting dingers to the moon.

The normal moon not the one from before that kills us all so slowly as it arrives.

Then I saw that they were sharing voicemails the president left for his son on TV for some reason. They had a graphic up of one that went something like "It's dad. I called to tell you I love you. I love you more than the whole world pal. You gotta get some help. I don't know what to do. I know you don't either."

I'm not sure what sort of point bringing that back up again is supposed to prove. That a guy loves his son? Find me a person in this country who hasn't said that sort of thing or else had it said to them by someone at some point in their life.

I want to say it right now to someone I love.

Maybe I want someone to say it to me too.

It would sure be nice if that president had always displayed such empathy for addicts or other suffering people throughout his career. Even ones he's not related to.

A very bad storm on the TV is a thousand miles away I just remembered.

I don't know why I've insisted upon bearing witness to this particular storm. I suppose it feels like a form of penance for my modest good fortune living for now outside of the biting circumference of a devastating hurricane's snapping beak.

Look at this goddamn guy my grandfather would say.

Did they even show storms on TV when I was young? Am I making that part up? I honestly do not know.

I was trying to remember something about my family earlier. My other grandfather my paternal grandfather was dead and in Hell before I was conscious of anything. He was either from Malden or Revere or Dorchester. The difference between those places doesn't mean anything to anyone besides the people who are from there.

The specifics of my maternal grandfather's personality – the guy I'm talking about looking at the storms with here – basically sifted through my grasp as I learned to learn what the world is like despite having spent time at his shaking foot. The integrity of our respective brains' functioning capacity racing in the opposite direction at the same time. Him regressing and me going toward what he wasn't ever going to be anymore.

My mother had three children by the age of twenty-one with my father. A fourth later on with my other father. The first of them was stolen away from her at fifteen years old and it just now at the age of forty five for the first time occurred to me that maybe that moment that singular defining moment of my mother's life also fucked him up too. Why didn't I ever think that? Not that it would excuse the abuse and the menacing that followed but what a weird thing just now just now just now just now to think that maybe he had claim to emotional damage over that theft when he was still a child himself as well.

We do love to reverse engineer motivation for abusive men I suppose but I feel like I would have come to that angle sooner.

I don't remember any of that either way and in any case it is not my problem. Not my most pressing problem anyway.

That sentence is one of the things that isn't true in here.

I saw some grade school buddies I still love recently and we sat around a fire and talked about the things you talk about with grade school buddies and unlike them I couldn't summon the name of one single teacher I had back then not even to make them laugh which is the one thing I care about doing for them and maybe the one thing I care about doing at all for anyone.

My new therapist is trying to tell me that all of that abuse and baby snatching and wife beating led to post traumatic what have you for me but I was two or three or four at the time and who remembers what anything was like at that age. I barely remember being thirty at this point. What would I have been thinking about on any given day back then? Conquering the world I suppose. The misgivings of thirty year old men. One of the most evil ages a man can be.

The only job I remember my grandmother having was "working at the phone company" and after all of that she just flounced around a derelict farmhouse with the poisoned corn fields in the back casting spells on all of us to give us eating disorders and posture dysphoria if that's a thing.

Look at this guy standing in the wind I said just now to no one. It might have even been the same asshole from back when my grandfather was alive for all I knew. It was him now that I looked closer. They let these guys go on working forever. What other job after this are they qualified for?

They poured this guilt into me. Less like a type of compassion than vainglory. How all distant suffering was mine to collect on at a later date. A man coveting a beautiful car or woman he thinks he is owed but he knows will destroy him eventually. Or how guilt is sustenance. A meager gruel to be sure but when the land happens to be well suited to grow wheat or potatoes the people cultivate wheat or potatoes. And are proud of the wheat or potatoes subsequently. Look how deeply we've plowed the field.

The rain just started up here in earnest and it lashed the window and startled me like a thrown water balloon connecting with my face.

Who did that?

Looking around for the juvenile culprit giggling no doubt now behind a bush.

The storm's violence bored me at last so I looked at my phone again and read a quote from another writer who said something like "Hope is not optimism, which expects things to turn out well, but something rooted in the conviction that there is good worth working for."

I don't know if I fully believe that at the moment. Sometimes I do because you have to. Then again I just saw that Tom DeLonge is back in Blink-182 and they're going on tour so maybe that's the sort of thing he meant.

Get inside dummy my grandfather would yell.

We can all see the extent of the storm without someone posing in it my grandfather would say but maybe the idea behind it all with the guy in the rain is like how you can never fully comprehend how hurting someone you love will actually look until you see them standing there in the middle of their destruction. They can't walk or speak normally anymore from the pummeling. Every previously mundane task now a heroic lift for them to accomplish and you have to force yourself to watch. To shave off a tiny portion of their ordeal and feel it dissolve in your hand like grasped seaspray. To at least understand the basics of what it will feel like when it's your turn.

Luke O'Neil is the author of the acclaimed political and literary newsletter Welcome to Hell World and the book of the same name. His collection of short fiction and poetry, *A Creature Wanting Form*, was published in 2023. He's a former writer-at-large for *Esquire* and was a longtime journalist for *The Boston Globe*, *The Guardian*, and many other newspapers and magazines. He was born and will likely die in Massachusetts.

Printed and bound by CPI Group (UK) Ltd, Croydon, CR0 4YY

24/09/2025

01961873-0004